LEGACY OF GOLD

A Novel by

Raphael Sackville

Melbourne's first synagogue, dedicated in 1848.

TARGUM / FELDHEIM

First published 1989

ISBN 0-944070-19-1

Phototypeset at Targum Press

Published by:
Targum Press Inc.
22700 W. Eleven Mile Rd.
Southfield, Mich. 48034

Distributed by:
Philipp Feldheim Inc.
200 Airport Executive Park
Spring Valley, N.Y. 10977

Distributed in Israel by:
Nof Books Ltd.
POB 23646
Jerusalem 91235

Printed in Israel

To my loving parents,
for their endless support, trust, and patience.

THE TORAH OF YOUR MOUTH
IS BETTER TO ME THAN
THOUSANDS OF GOLD AND SILVER

(*TEHILLIM* 119:72)

A Note to the Reader

Many of the events that take place in *Legacy of Gold* are historically accurate. Faced with a shortage of space in her penitentiaries early in the nineteenth century, England converted the newly discovered land of Australia into one large prison. Among the countless thousands sent out by ship were numerous Jewish unfortunates, some of them falsely accused, others convicted of crimes such as stealing a loaf of bread to feed a starving family.

In the early 1850s, John Dunlop, an aging gold miner, found the largest goldfield in Australia, at Ballarat. This led to the obsessive delirium that came to be known as the gold rush years.

Many of the characters appearing in the book did actually live through this exciting time. Moses Rintel was appointed to lead the Melbourne Hebrew Congregation and married into the well-respected Hart family.

Asher Hart and his cousin Henri played an instrumental part in consolidating the small number of Jews in Melbourne at the time; until the appointment of a *chazzan* and Torah reader, Asher Hart himself carried out these duties. Before sailing to Melbourne, John Henry Anderson was the secretary of the Launceston Hebrew Congregation in Tasmania, a large island south of Australia. Walter Lindenthal worked with a few Jewish communities as *chazzan*, while Samuel Isaacs and Solomon Benjamin were leading members of both the Jewish and general Melbourne community.

No remains exist of Cashmore's Corner or the synagogue built at the top of Bourke Street, Melbourne, though both institutions did exist at the time.

Though I have used these true-life figures as minor characters, the part they play in this novel is wholly fictitious and is solely a product of my imagination. All other characters in the book are fictitious and any resemblance they may have to known personalities is purely coincidental.

Raphael G. R. Sackville
Jerusalem, 1989

Prologue

The bearded young man stood by the postal window fingering the carefully wrapped package that had been placed before him. The clerk, seeing the bemused expression on the young man's face, quickly asked him if everything was in order.

"Oh...oh, yes," the young man answered in heavily accented Hebrew.

"In that case—" the postal clerk nodded meaningfully in the direction of the line of impatient people awaiting his attention.

With an apologetic smile, the young man moved to the side of the main Jerusalem post office. Again, he stared at the brown paper, the neatly tied string, and, especially, the postmark. Melbourne! It had been years since he had lived in his Australian hometown, years since his family, upset with his decision to live as an Orthodox Jew, had cast him adrift.

He himself hadn't realized how much he'd felt his lack of roots, of continuity, of family, not until that day several months ago when he'd received the first unexpected letter from Melbourne. The elegant stationary bore the name of one of Australia's most respected law firms.

The letter itself was a puzzle:

> Mr. Moshe Lazar
> Maalot Dafna, Jerusalem, Israel
>
> Dear Mr. Lazar:
>
> Pursuant to the terms of the last will and testament of the late Moses Lazar, upon receipt of proof of identity and a letter affirming your present status as a student in a religious institution in Jerusalem, a bequest will be forwarded. Your reply is awaited.

A bequest from whom? For what? How much?

"I don't believe it," he thought. "But then, again, why not? Stranger things have happened." He was aware that his forebears had been wealthy. Perhaps a legacy had come his way from some forgotten great-uncle.

He went, almost on a whim, to the office of his yeshiva, a respected institution for *ba'alei teshuvah*, got the letter certifying his student status requested by the lawyers, and sent it off with a copy of his birth certificate, passport, and a notarized letter from the Australian consulate. Then he forgot about it—until yesterday, when he'd received the postal notice. A parcel, sent via registered mail, was awaiting him.

And now, before him, lay the mysterious box with that compelling, evocative postmark: Melbourne.

Moshe walked slowly down Rechov Yaffo, clutching the package. As he waited at the crowded bus stop, he impulsively ripped it open. The Jerusalem sun glinted sharply upon...gold! A golden menorah! Startled, he quickly covered it again and carefully drew out the other object. It was a journal, leather-bound, with words carefully gold-stamped upon it.

The Chronicle of Moses Lazar
1879

Moses Lazar...Moshe Lazar...

He couldn't wait for the bus; he hailed a taxi and raced home.

Inside his small apartment he carefully took out the contents of the mysterious package.

In front of him stood the menorah. It was blackened in places, but otherwise hadn't suffered over time. He couldn't take his eyes off it. Its every curve had been made with such loving, meticulous care. He supposed that its value would run into thousands of dollars. He picked it up. It measured from the end of his middle finger to mid-forearm.

He had the urge to polish it, but his hand instinctively reached out to the leather-bound volume lying in front of him. The menorah could wait. He placed a small coffee table in front of his most comfortable armchair and rested the menorah on top of it close enough to touch while he read. He took the manuscript in hand and studied it carefully.

It was larger than the size of a magazine and bound in thick, camel brown leather. It opened with what appeared to be an introduction.

Though eager to start reading, Moshe couldn't bring himself to begin until he had leafed through the thick, cream-colored pages. This was his manuscript, and yet he still didn't feel as though it belonged to him. He wanted to feel its texture, let its leathery aroma permeate the air with its musty smell of the past.

At last he was ready. He thumbed carefully back to the introduction and began to read.

I have done nothing singular in this life of mine to warrant my name's enduring after I leave this world. Many years from now the memory of my name and the turmoil of the years I shall soon write of will be forgotten. I have never chased nor cared for fame, and have made it my business to live a simple, honest life and do my utmost to avoid controversy. My life, however, has been filled with everything but the quiet I have sought. I confess that it has had more twists and turns to it than I can count or wish to remember.

I have been transformed quite overnight from a member of the poor rabble of England to the ranks of the newfound aristocracy of Australia. Today I am able to afford whatever my heart desires. My family and I lack nothing. There is not an item or piece of land existing in this colony that I could not obtain should I so desire. My reward in this world has been huge, and I only pray that I shall have merited reward in the next world as well.

Rich though I am, I enter the twilight years of my life an unhappy man. My nights are sleepless and my days somber. My time in this world is not measured by minutes and hours, but by a fear that has bound me like a man shackled in chains.

I was born a Jew and shall die one, proud that the law Moses brought down from Sinai has been revered, respected, and kept by me to the best of my limited ability. But I am only one man, and my sphere of influence has fallen low. I see those Jewish souls living around me losing touch with the law given to us 3,191 years ago.

I cannot blame them. Here in Australia, thousands of miles from the closed life of sullen England, we live in a land of endless, empty plains, among a foreign people. Our numbers are small. We haven't the means to educate our children, feed our families, and honor our God as we have been commanded. We have become like the nations who flock to these shores whether by free choice or not. Today we live alongside them as neighbors. Tomorrow our families shall assimilate into theirs. Then all will be lost. I pray to the Almighty every day that He spare my family until the Messiah comes to redeem us so we may have the honor to continue worshiping the Lord with total devotion.

Such is my lot: a lonely Jew condemned to live out the remainder of his days dreaming of the holy Jerusalem that he shall never see.

When I have finished this story I shall entrust it to my solicitor with strict instructions that it remain sealed until such time that a descendant of mine shall study in the holy city itself. To him, and him alone, I shall entrust my story. My prayer is that my words will bring inspiration to a heart that has already turned to face the Almighty in His holiest of cities. I am not naive. I realize that I may not succeed and three generations hence ours may be a family totally lost. If this should happen, God forbid, then my story shall remain a secret forever. Yet somewhere deep in my heart I know that many years from now a descendant of mine will have found the merit to read these pages.

Child of my future, pray with me now that the flame of perfection in this world that our forefathers lit never be extinguished. Let us pray that the menorah light shall once again find its place in the next Beis Hamikdash.

Chazak VeAmatz,

Moses Lazar
Melbourne, 1879

Chapter 1

I will never forget the stench that permeated the bowels of the freezing hulk called the *Havring* as it sailed me out of England, away from my starving family. It increased in intensity with every mile that further distanced my fellow unfortunates and myself from the docks of Portsmouth, until finally, upon reaching the shores of Australia, we had become like the disgusting filth itself—nothing more than refuse that required dumping. And that is what we were: human refuse traveling across the seas to the largest natural prison in the world.

Ah, the *Havring*! Cruel, cruel ship that she was. It was she who tore me away from my dear wife, son, and daughter. It was she who showed me the sights of the world through her gloomy portholes—the Canary Islands, Cape Verde Islands, Rio De Janeiro, Cape Town, and further eastward until we were spewed out at Port

Philip Bay on the southeast coast of Australia.

The voyage took three months, and many a strong man died along the way. Indeed, many died before we even left port, be it from heartbreak or exposure to the cold weather of England.

My fellow passengers were, in the main, poor men turned to crime for the purpose of feeding their starving families. I can recall one young boy no older than ten who had joined our ranks for the crime of having stolen a handkerchief from the pocket of a gentleman. That "gentleman," who probably lived like a lord in London, surely didn't own enough handkerchiefs to soak up the tears that the poor boy's family shed on the docks as we sailed away.

Our punishments were severe, seven or fourteen years banishment to Australia. I had been sentenced to seven years for allegedly stealing half a pound of flour. The magistrate in his drunken duty passed judgment over me in a fleeting instant.

"Your crime, Jew," spoke the red-faced drunkard, "deserves more than the seven years I'm giving you. You're a shame to the Queen and your people. Yet seven years should see you an honest man again."

We were stuffed, overcrowded and freezing, into the holds of the old warship one cold February morning in 1849. The ship had been crudely converted to accommodate more men than she could handle. In the darkness of the holds we were each designated a plank to lie on, and in such fashion we left Portsmouth.

To prepare us for our voyage we were clipped by

the ship's barber. I could see him eyeing my *peyos* from a distance. When I came before him he smiled cunningly. "Well, if we don't have one of the chosen before us. Show me your locks then, Jew." He grabbed first one, then the other, and shore them off with a curse.

When it came my turn to receive the ship's uniform, the quartermaster tried to snatch the *tallis* and *tefillin* which I had miraculously managed to hold on to since my sentencing, but I held fast to the precious bundle. He was a brute of a man, and I was certain he'd beat me for my insolence. I had watched as he poked his knife through each article of clothing of the men before me, keeping whatever he thought valuable enough to sell for profit. His knife tore into the *tallis* covering the *tefillin*. He cursed me, spat at my feet, and sent me along the line.

"On with yer, Jew! Yer can have yer things, but I'll wager my privilegin' it will do yer more evil than good."

And by his lights he was right. Their presence brought me derision and attempted physical abuse. Yet without them I'm sure I would have perished along with the others.

I originally believed, and rather naively, that having been torn away from our loved ones and the country of our birth, we wretches might bond in brotherhood. Nothing could have been further removed from the truth. The weak were preyed upon by the strong, the gentle by the cunning. We Jews have always brought attention upon ourselves, and I was no exception. With my *peyos* shorn and the clothes torn off my back, still they knew I was a Jew—and that was ammunition enough for them. The most wicked among them ruled the holds below, and their violence knew no bounds.

HaKadosh Baruch Hu created me unusually large and strong, in itself a miracle considering the poverty I came from. Perhaps I was so created to sustain me on the *Havring*'s passage. There were times when I was set upon by more than a few of them. When they attacked me I fought like a pariah dog, until I had nearly mauled them all. All this to protect my objects of faith and my dignity.

I stood out for other reasons, too. I never ate the dry meat flung at us by our jailers. The officers got used to me and would deride me by offering me double rations amid waves of raucous laughter.

The ringleader, a man called Jack O'Hearn, would often shout from across the galley that he wished he were a Jew so he could fill his belly on my Jew's double portion.

I didn't starve though. We were given lime juice, sugar, and vinegar against scurvy. There was rice, pudding, and peas. Though of course these weren't kosher either, after two days of fasting I decided that for reasons of *pikuach nefesh*, saving my life, I would eat just enough to sustain me. I drew the line, however, with meat—and can proudly say that the taste of *treife* meat has never passed these lips of mine. With my belly half full I was able to survive in what I thought a better frame of body than the men who ate that rotted pork.

Jack O'Hearn was the toughest man I have ever set eyes on. He used to beat anyone in sight, including the officers who came to feed us. It was early in the passage when he paid a call on me. Until then I had never fought a man. A Jew, after all, is raised for better things than brawling. Yet I fought O'Hearn for my life, and he received as much of a thrashing as I did. Never again after that occasion did he approach me for a fight. I could tell I had wounded his Irish pride, and yet I found that he came to respect me in his typical insolent manner. He'd insult me, but there was always a glint of veiled respect in his eye when he did. And no man could curse like Jack O'Hearn.

Using brute strength against another has never come to me easily. I have only used it as a last resort, when my very life was at stake. We Jews are a God-loving people who shy from such brutish exercise. I can honestly say that every time I have had to resort to fighting I have regretted it, wishing a gentle word in the other man's ear was all that was needed to settle differences. Alas! Men not educated by Torah have yet to learn this valuable lesson.

For his insolence O'Hearn was flogged with the cat-o'-nine-tails on many an occasion. The "cat" had a long leather-bound handle from which hung nine strips of thick hide. The ends of each were knotted twice. Before being used in a flogging, they were soaked in seawater, to add what the head officer called "a little sting to hear you sing by." Hardened men like O'Hearn, and there were many, refused to sing. If they were flogged twenty-five or two hundred times they never once raised their voices to complain or cry out in pain.

We were made to watch the proceedings, which took place on deck. I vividly recall one particular flogging, a ghastly affair. Standing before us, tied to the triangle, O'Hearn turned to the ship's captain, looked him in the eye, and said, "I cannot help it. I was born a wild man. I will rebel against your likes again and again and never be broken by your treachery." He spat at the captain's feet and then yelled at the flogger. "Put your back and shoulder into it or you're a coward if ever there was one."

Once the beating was over, we were sent back down to the hatches. For his troubles O'Hearn's back was doused in seawater.

Davening Shacharis was the greatest hurdle I had to overcome on the passage. Every morning I'd wake before the other men and say my morning prayers. The only shame that I felt was having to pray in that pigsty. What alternative was there for me? I'd stand defiant and proud as the men were woken at reveille.

"You'd be better hanging yourself by them straps than wrapping them round your arm." Such was the daily comment I heard from the wizened old pickpocket who slept next to me, by the name of Burling, the first words he spoke every morning.

The abuse hurled at me every day paled in comparison to what I received on Shabbos.

"Jew Lazar! What makes this day different from the

others we've spent in this hole?" O'Hearn would shout at me. "What good's your Jew God helping you in the middle of these seas? Wear your straps today or tomorrow, it will make you no difference. Us scum don't have the right to nothin'. Not even a God. So what makes you different from the likes of us, then? Chosen? All you were chosen for, Jew Lazar, was the scum heap of the world. That's all your Father in heaven chose you for."

Strange as it may seem, I recall those torrents of abuse with pride. I found the courage to withstand their curses and maintain my dignity. Today I actually find it amusing that there are non-Jews living in this colony who know that Jews don't put on *tefillin* on Shabbos. They learned that from Jew Lazar.

If there was any small comfort to be taken on the *Havring* it was the thought that those above deck were suffering, too. Apart from the human cargo below, there were voyagers on their way to Australia, "free immigrants" who were going to try their luck across the seas. They were made welcome in the colony for their capital or skills. Thousands made their passage that year and in the years following, mainly because England's economic depression sent them searching for fairer pastures.

Finally, after months at sea, Port Philip Bay came into view. I remember the seas being particularly choppy that day and the winds unusually fierce. It was raining, although in comparison to the cold, wet London winter, the temperature was mild.

Our docking caused quite an uproar. We filed out

of our holds onto the quay. To an observer we must have looked a dishevelled, unimpressive lot. Many well-to-do men, colonial officers, and sightseers gathered to watch us disembark. We were greeted, if such a word is appropriate, by a self-important man by the name of Grey. He addressed us in a loud voice, intending, no doubt, of making certain that the spectators gathered there could hear his every word. He was a man who liked to create impressions. He informed us that though we had been exiled from England, we had much to look forward to in Australia if we applied ourselves to the task at hand. There was work a'plenty waiting to be allotted to us, and should we prove ourselves trustworthy and adhere carefully to the laws of our imprisonment, we could look forward to early emancipation and the right to work as free men.

As I mentioned earlier, I am a large man. I stood head and shoulders above most of the men, and as a result must have drawn attention to myself. I soon saw a man, who looked quite a gentleman, busily speaking to the officer standing directly behind Grey. Another officer sent to our ranks told me to step out of line. The gentleman approached and looked me over from head to toe. I felt like a slave at an auction.

"What are you carrying there, man?" he asked me, pointing to the bundle that never left my possession.

"I'm a Jew. I pray with these," I answered.

"Can you be trusted, Jew?"

"To trust you?" I replied defiantly. The man broke into raucous laughter.

"I like a humorous fellow," he said. "Listen, Jew. I'm going to give you a choice. You can go with the others and work for Her Majesty or come and work for me. If you are interested, I can arrange for you to be separated from this mob forever. And let me warn you that your chances of finding a master as gentle as I are as remote as the forgotten shores of England."

"What makes you interested in me?" I asked.

"Look at you! You're a giant compared to the others. A bit of good food in you and you'll do the work of three men. Well then, are you interested?"

"I'm interested. But I want the right to practice living as a Jew."

He broke into laughter again. "Jew, you are in no position to make demands. Were you let loose among some of the livelier residents in this fair colony, you'd be quickly torn to shreds," he laughed.

"I survived the holds of the *Havring* for three months at sea and I see no reason I shouldn't do the same on land," I replied.

Being as ignorant as any newly convicted man on foreign shores, I saw treachery in everything. I was as willing to go with him as not, and so had drawn him out to bargain, knowing full well that whichever way I turned I was taking risks. I looked him in the eye. He stared back and, after a moment, said, "It's either a foolish or brave man who plays cards the way you do. I'll give you your freedom to practice your faith as a Jew, and you'll work for me as I demand or I'll turn you loose upon the dogs of this town."

"So be it," I said.

"What's your name then, good Jew?"

"Lazar. Moses Lazar."

"My name's George Matthews." He motioned me to stay where I was and walked toward the officers overseeing us.

While he was gone, I couldn't help but think about the family I'd left behind. We had no means of communication, no hope of seeing each other for years. I was alone, with no one but Hashem. Had any Jew since the destruction of the great Temple ever been this deep into exile?

Like tormented Jews throughout the ages, I stood praying to the Lord to spare my dear family and not make their suffering too great a burden to bear. I prayed with a broken heart that Hashem, in His glory, sound the shofar for our freedom and gather us, His exiles, from the four corners of the earth. "*Te'kah beshofar gadol lecheruseinu...*"

"Open your eyes, Lazar," came the command. "There's no time for dreaming. We've lost half a day already and I'll be loathe to waste the other half on account of your idleness."

George Matthews had returned, holding the required documents. He waved them victoriously. Suddenly I felt as if I'd been sold into bondage. The reality of my sentence was beginning to sink in.

Matthews was in his mid-thirties, medium in height, and heavyset. From a distance he looked quite fierce, although I was soon to discover his nature was compassionate. He was dressed in the height of fashion, from the immaculately polished and shining riding boots to the brushed felt hat on his head. I had no idea what Matthews had in store for me, and quite honestly I didn't care. But I found myself following him out of the port, as a dog follows its master, into the blustery Melbourne afternoon.

I walked behind him at a distance of a couple of yards until we came to a carriage. There were no servants to meet us, just two horses hitched to a cart, their heads buried deeply in nosebags. "Welcome to Melbourne, Mr. Lazar," announced Matthews. "The city of gamblers, drunkards, rioters, and hell on earth. In this colonial outpost you'll find neither roads nor railways leading off to the other colonies. We have no telegraph system, and the only attachment we have to mother England is twelve thousand miles of ocean. This is your new home, good Jew Lazar, and if you'll be seeking ways out of here, let me inform you that there are two: death or obedience. The former is common and occurs constantly. The latter is granted to a man who works hard and honestly. Give me a year of solid work and I'll give you the freedom you want. Come then, Lazar," he said, as he took the nosebags off the horses. "Our time is short and there's much work to be done."

I climbed into the carriage and sat down next to him. He flicked the reins sharply and off we trotted to my as yet unknown destination.

Matthews was in a rush. He whipped the horses

forward, but our progress was hindered by the terrible conditions of the roads. Rains had transformed the dirt roads into bogs, and the danger of sinking into the morass was ever present. I had no real interest in learning where we were going. My thoughts were far away, in London. I barely listened as Matthews talked.

"I've been granted property just west of the city. I've a run of sheep there. We're in the process of building the fences that pen the sheep in at night. With a little luck, this country should prove a sheep owner's gold mine. Others have seen success. I hope my choice of land will see me as wealthy.

"Look here, Lazar," he said, emphasizing the point, "if I don't make a fair go of this run, I'm a finished man. I need decent, honest men to make it work. The last man I employed ran off as soon as he'd money enough in his pockets to drink a gallon of rum. Do you drink?"

"I can get by on a small cup a week," I answered, thinking to myself that if no other drink was available, I'd use spirits for making kiddush on Shabbos morning.

"One cup, you say?" he laughed. "What sort of cup do you have in mind?"

"A cup's a cup over here as much as it is over in England, I guess," I replied.

"Men become wild when they're filled with the devil's drink."

"You don't like a drink?" I asked. Hearing this, Matthews laughed so hard he nearly fell out of the carriage.

"I didn't know my question was that funny, Mr. Matthews."

"Ah, rum! Without rum my nights would be sober, and if they were, Jew Lazar, I'd be driven to madness. Have a look under the canvas behind you." I turned around, lifted the canvas, and saw three large barrels of rum. And then, as if to remind me of his real intent, he declared, "But my days are for work. D'you hear, man?"

As the roads became increasingly difficult to traverse, we spoke less. We passed through the main settlement, Melbourne, and were traveling over rough country. The land was flat and dull, the few hills slightly undulating. Looking up I was amazed by the color of the sky. It was unlike the sky of England, a deeper, richer blue, a color that gave off an encouraging light. For the first time, I felt a promise of something brighter than the squalid life I'd left behind in England. I thought of my family, reflecting as I did on the awful circumstances that had led me to misery and a ticket to the other side of the world.

Chapter 2

I was born in 1820, the year King George IV began his reign, the only son of Yaakov and Tziporah Lazar. My father served as *shammas* in one of the many small shuls of London, and both my parents were tailors.

During the time of King George's reign, every man was looking for employment, for a way to feed his family. Almost overnight the number of people living in London increased a thousandfold. The reason for this influx into the city was what later came to be known as the Industrial Revolution. At the turn of the century, most of the people in England lived on the land. With the Industrial Revolution, the starving people of England's farmlands flocked like sheep to the major industrial cities for the promise of jobs in the new factories. With little room available for them, they were, in the main, cramped into hovels, living hard, bitter lives.

We lived in Stepney, which, together with Whitechapel, was home to most of the city's Jews. The living conditions there were utterly revolting. We were housed one on top of the other in horribly crowded quarters. Raw sewage ran through the streets, home to armies of mice and rats larger than cats, that kept us constantly on watch. Our food was never safe around them; were we to leave food on our plates longer than a moment or two, we'd find these abominable creatures making a banquet.

We Jews weren't the only ones doomed to a life of misery. Most of the surrounding areas of London were just as poorly off. The gap that existed between the rich and poor was enormous. Lords and gentlemen grew fatter every day from the wealth that their factories created, while we suffered and lived the lives of beasts of burden. This was the irony of life in Georgian England.

When I was a lad of fifteen, my father died. He didn't suffer from prolonged sickness. He started his last day as he always did: he awoke at dawn and spent two hours davening and learning. Then he came home and began work tailoring the latest orders, usually military uniforms. Just before lunch he said he didn't feel well. He went to his bed for a rest and never got up again.

My father was a wonderful teacher who constantly impressed upon me the importance of Torah study. He left an enormous emptiness in my life when he left the world.

Death was so prevalent in Georgian England that it wasn't uncommon to find corpses lying in streets. If it wasn't the working conditions that helped shorten one's life, it was the diseases for which there were no cures to be found anywhere—unless, of course, you had money to buy one.

My mother aged rapidly after my father's passing under the full burden of responsibility that lay on her slim shoulders. She, too, suffered in the Georgian Age. Working as a military tailor was no job of ease. The constant sewing in the dim light of our home caused her eyes to water continuously and lose their sight. By the time I was seventeen she was nearly blind and ineffective as a worker.

So the burden of living fell upon my shoulders. I had been blessed by Hashem with sharpness of mind, and since my father had taught me to read and write in English, I found work when my mother fell ill. Not many boys my age had these skills; the majority were thrown out to work at an early age, sometimes at five or six. Not only could I master the English word but the Hebrew language as well.

My writing skills found me employment as a clerk for a man of trade. My job was to write out documents. The work brought home money enough to make our lives sufferable. At the end of the day I would come home and help my mother and her helper, a girl called Rachel, finish off any orders that remained after my father's death.

Eighteen hundred and forty, the year of my

marriage to Rachel and my mother's death, was a difficult time for all of England. There was less work to be found then than in living memory, and as a result, many men and women took to lives of crime. The system of justice in Georgian times was appalling. Not one convicted man in a hundred would have been found guilty by a Jewish court of law. Murder, although not uncommon, was regarded by the law as a crime of secondary importance, whereas crimes against property were regarded as the greatest offenses possible against the King. One could steal a chicken, a stocking, or a loaf of bread and be sent to Tyburn, the place for public execution, to be hanged.

And hang men they did. I can remember a year when over 150 men and women went over the drop at Tyburn. A hanging was an event to which thousands of people flocked to watch. They cheered as the convicted man was led in a horse-drawn cart through the streets. If he were well liked, flowers and praise were heaped upon him. If he were a rogue whom the common people disliked, he'd be pelted with food and stones. The law made an effort to publicize hangings in the hope they'd repulse people enough to turn them away from a life of crime.

After witnessing my first hanging I was scared out of my wits and swore I'd never resort to doing anything against the law. For weeks all I dreamed about was the fight that took place after the hanging, as the dead man's family fought in vain against those hard-bitten men who took bodies to sell for profit.

My wife and I were very happy with each other despite the hardships, but our happiness was shattered a year after our wedding when she nearly died in childbirth. The child died soon after seeing the light of this world. It took months for Rachel to regain her strength, and when she did she wasn't as she had been before her confinement.

With harder times upon us, our income dwindled to a pitiable sum. I found it necessary to stop learning in the synagogue at nights, as I'd done for years, in order to gain extra work.

In 1844, Rachel gave birth to twins. We named the boy Yaakov and the girl Rivkah. Although the winter was harsh and freezing, somehow they survived. They were, and still are, beautiful children who give us much *nachas*.

During the days before Rosh Hashanah of 1848, an event occurred that changed the course of all our lives. On the way home from my night work, I would sometimes loiter longer than I should have around the local bakeries in the hope of buying some cheap flour. As luck had it, I sometimes found a *metziah* here or there—nothing to make a feast out of, but enough, nonetheless, to make small loaves of bread.

Though our lot saddened us, it was better than starvation. My wife and I knew that there was little hope of improving our situation—these were the facts of life in mother England.

My scavenger hunts had continued for a few years, until that eventful Friday. It was the eve of the New

Year, and we were poorer than usual. After I paid the landlord, there was little left in my pocket. The Yom Tov was soon to begin and we still hadn't the money to purchase flour to make the festive loaves. Rather than take a pinch here and there from our neighbors, who often didn't have enough for themselves, I went out from work, hoping to find some cheap flour.

I entered a bakery that I usually passed on my way home. It was full of customers, and the shop people were busy with trade. I moved to the side of the shop, where several bags of flour rested. I drew the attention of a baker I knew and asked if there were any bargains to be had.

"Sorry, Moses. Not an ounce of flour to give you," was all he could say to me.

A young man, well noted in the area for his ability to steal, edged in next to me. I watched as he deftly sliced into the top of a sack with a knife, put his hand into it, and stealthily filled his jacket pocket, which was lined with a piece of cloth, with flour. This couldn't have taken longer than a few seconds. When I noticed what he was doing I grabbed his hand tightly. Rather than take fright at my actions, he looked at me in disgust. His hands were quicker than mine, and in an instant he was free. Then he cried out aloud:

"Thief! This man's stealing flour."

There was a momentary hush in the shop, and then the shopkeeper, a hefty man with a short temper, made his way through the crowd to where I stood.

"Thief? Come man. Turn your pockets out."

Seeing I had nothing to fear, I put my hands in my pockets as he had requested. To my horror, I found the same flour-filled cloth the ruffian had laced into his pocket. I protested, pointing out that the other bakers knew me as an honest man, pleading that I was no thief. I turned to where the real thief had stood a moment before, but he had fled.

The Lord's Commandments have always rung loudly in my ears. Thou Shall Not Steal. Had I transgressed one of the Commandments? No! I was being wrongly accused of theft, and there was nothing I could do to stop the dangerous wheels of fate that had begun to turn. From that moment on, I was a condemned man. My heart sank. I knew what lay in wait for me.

The pain I felt for my beloved wife and children nearly drove me insane. It became evident that I wouldn't be spending the New Year with my family or in the synagogue. They dragged me to Newgate Prison where I was locked up like a wild animal.

Newgate Prison was hell on earth. No hardship I'd ever endured came close to what went on behind those cruel walls. Upon entering I had a spiked chain placed around my neck, which nearly choked me to death. The warden threatened he'd tighten it should I not pay for the board they were offering. I discovered later that this was the usual process the prison employed to acquire money.

I had nothing in my pockets. After I was caught, every bit of flour and anything else that could be found there was taken from me. In my life I've had a lot of luck, and the first occasion I recall its providence upon me was in Newgate. One of the men who was attempting to squeeze money and breath out of me left the room. He returned with another man, who looked at me in disgust and said, "No use in asking any of them to come down and pay his keep. The sun's setting and one of their praying days is about to begin. Wilbers has five Jews working for him, and he told me there was nothing he could do or say to get them to work until Monday."

With that he left the room, and the chains were taken from around my neck. I was led into a ward where they kept those they locked up. The smell of the room was unbearable, and I was all but totally overcome. There was no discrimination as to who was thrown into these wards. There were young boys no older than eight, men of every age and description, and women as well. The deplorable activities that I was a witness to I will not attempt to describe; I only wish I could erase them from my mind. In Newgate there was no escaping the worst forms of human behavior. I couldn't believe that England had become so degraded.

I spent five days and nights locked up in Newgate until I was dragged before the magistrate hearing my case. Nothing I said led them to think differently of me. I was made aware that I was lucky to have escaped the hangman. The Jews in our district had "done business" with the magistrate and had made as certain as they possibly could that I would be spared the hangman's noose. The second best punishment His Majesty's law could provide would be handed down to me instead.

The magistrate was a red-faced drunkard whose self-importance was by far the dominant factor of my trial, a mock performance that took no longer than two minutes. I can still recall the magistrate's final comments.

"I sentence you to seven years hard labor in Australia. You ought to be thankful that His Majesty has had mercy on you. You should be swinging from a rope instead. Now go and mend your ways."

I was placed in chains and taken to Portsmouth, together with a gang of convicted unfortunates. We were told that our trip to penal servitude was at hand. Until that fateful day, the docks of Portsmouth would be our home.

When my wife found out where I was, she came down to see me. It was difficult talking to her, and I'll never forget the broken look she wore when her eyes met mine.

"Oh, Moses," she cried. "Being too honest has led you to no good. Why didn't you leave that youth alone? Now you're leaving me and the children forever."

I tried my best to calm her. I swore that I'd come back at the first opportunity. If I wasn't able to return I'd work hard enough to bring her and the children across. This made her cry all the more. I begged her not to lose hope, telling her that God's help was swift and sure.

I knew that our community of good Jews would see to my wife and children's care. There was not much else to do other than encourage her with hope.

Traveling to Portsmouth was an ordeal and taxed her strength greatly. I told her to come but one more time to bring my *tallis* and *tefillin*. She looked at me, amazed. I didn't stand the remotest chance of keeping them, she said. She'd heard stories about the passage to Australia, how theft and murder were common among the men. Why should I bring unwarranted attention to myself by wearing *tallis* and *tefillin*?

I was a hard man to dissuade, and she was in no mood to argue with me. She carried with her an air of fatality. She was sure as the sun rose that she'd never hear or see me again. And so when she came to visit me for the last time in November of 1848, she carried the *tallis* and *tefillin* with her. She had left the children at home with her parents. She was more depressed than the first visit, and again I tried my best to show a strong face. But how could I? I was as broken as she. I knew nothing about Australia or what life lay ahead for me there. I was in no position to assure her when, or if, we'd see each other again.

Our parting was the most painful blow I was ever dealt. I watched as she walked away, her shoulders bent over and heaving with sobs. I cried a broken man's tears that day on the docks of Portsmouth. It was after I had no more tears to cry that I resigned myself to the unsure life awaiting me.

Winter was approaching quickly and the *Havring* didn't sail as planned. From what I could make out, there were differences between the owners of the ship and the ship's captain. We were housed in the open, and until we finally sailed in February, many men died on the docks from the cold. I only prayed that somewhere in faraway Australia I'd come across other Jews and finally find the means to either sail back or ship my family out.

It was thinking about the Jews that lived in the colony that brought me back to my carriage ride with George Matthews.

"Mr. Matthews," I asked, "are there any Jews in the settlement of Melbourne?"

"Jews?" He looked surprised, even embarrassed, by my question. "Not many. But they're an active lot. When we next travel into Melbourne I'll take you to see Hart the auctioneer."

"Who's he?" I inquired.

"Asher Hyman Hart. Used to be a draper but turned to auctioneering after his premises were burnt to a cinder."

"Are there any others?"

"A good few." He paused a moment, then continued. "Tell me, Lazar, about your wanting to keep your Jewish faith. Your demands are light, I hope."

"I won't work on our Sabbath, which isn't Sunday as you keep, rather Saturday. There are other holidays I'll want keeping. I'll give you notice a month before they're due."

"That's fine with me as long as you work Sundays."

"I will work Sundays," I answered.

"Is that it?" he said, looking at me with a cautious glance.

"Let me cook my own food. If there's any meat to be had I'll only eat it if I do the killing. I'll make sure I won't allow my praying hours to disturb my work. That's all."

"Doesn't sound too unreasonable," he muttered.

I had the feeling I was getting my way too easily. Maybe it was the suspicion I held for everything I saw. Yet Matthews genuinely appeared concerned only about his sheep run. I had no reason not to work hard for him. It wasn't as if I could steal his carriage from him, turn it around, and point it towards England. I simply had to bide my time, hoping as I did that my honesty and hard work would find me the chance to see my family once again.

We had come to the top of a hill, and here he stopped his carriage. He pointed westward towards his property. I saw a few small cabins situated in the middle of hundreds of square miles of pasture land. Then, just before reining his horses down the hill, Matthews turned to me and said, "Lazar, I've three men working for me and they're an incorrigible bunch. Two of them were sent out from England like you. The other is a free man. I came to the docks today looking for a special kind of man. I chose you for three reasons. First, I need a worker not afraid to put his shoulders into what he does. Second, I need a man I can trust. And third, I need a person who can organize my rowdy bunch.

"I've chosen you on nothing more than a hunch, but I believe you're fit for the job. You're free to practice as a Jew under me, but now you know what price it is I'm asking you to pay. Most of the men in this colony are only interested in escaping from their masters. I'm a fair man and have perhaps been too mild in the past. I'm desperate to succeed, and my entire fortune depends heavily on this run. Have you anything to say?" he ended, the laughter completely gone from his face.

"Why should an unruly crew listen to a man fresh from England?" I asked.

"Never you mind. You all speak the same language. You'll soon find you have plenty in common. My main concern is that your physical presence will be lesson enough for them."

"I'm not a fighting man, Mr. Matthews."

"Nor are they," he replied. "But you're a strong looking man. With a little food in you, no one will want to cross you. They'd run away from the first fist raised in their direction. I've said more than I intended. Have you anything to say?"

"No, Mr. Matthews. I'll give you my best."

"Then we've wasted enough time sitting here. Let's get down to work."

Once again he whipped the horses into a trot. His eyes were fixed straight ahead as if it were a dark tunnel he was leading his horses into. They snapped into a gallop under his rein, and it wasn't long before the property of George Matthews, landholder in the Western district of Port Philip, loomed large into view.

Chapter 3

The sun had nearly set as we rode into the station. No one greeted us as we pulled up in front of a row of three small shacks. Matthews made his way to the middle one and disappeared inside. He came out after a few moments and called across to me.

"The fire's burning. Take yourself a hot bath. There's a set of clothes that should fit you. When you've finished, you'll find your quarters in the last hut. I'll make sure to leave you some bread. If I can round up my men, they'll come to your room later to meet you. I don't think I've forgotten anything."

"If it's none too difficult, I'd be obliged if you could supply me with another undershirt and a needle and a cutting knife," I said.

"You've been given plenty, man. Be thankful you've fallen into my hands and no one else's."

With those parting words, Matthews disappeared

into the twilight. I walked into the shack excited by the prospect of my first hot bath in nearly six months. I quickly filled the tub with boiling water and was soon scrubbing myself down until my skin was nearly raw. I soaked for half an hour or so, washing myself again and again, trying to rid myself of the smell and feel of the *Havring*. After I was done, I dressed in the set of clothes Matthews had left me.

There was nothing singular about the room I'd been assigned to. It was small, furnished with a bed, a table, and a low bench. My instinct upon entering was to look for a mezuzah. I knew it was fruitless to pass my hand along the door frame, but did so anyway.

Mine was a sad situation. Here I was, occupying a room alone. In England, where most families lived eight to a room, this was unheard of. Often several families shared a room, partitioning them off and living like bees in a crowded colony. Here was a whole room for one man. It was a luxury I'd never known before, but it lacked one thing. My family!

The Almighty had His ways, I told myself. He wouldn't desert me even though I sat alone in Australia in the middle of a huge physical and spiritual wasteland. I had strong hopes that I would succeed in seeing my family again. Though others might deem my attitude naive, what other approach to life was there to take? That night I prayed with an uplifted heart.

When I was a boy, I used to watch my father pray. He would stand rigid, his hands firmly at his side, only his lips moving in prayer. Eyes closed, he would pray to the Almighty with total dedication. Like my father before me I, too, prayed—and still pray today—in the same manner.

When I reached *Shema* I spoke it loudly and distinctly. During *Shemoneh Esrei,* I felt the chains of the *Havring* removing themselves from my tormented soul. Long after I finished, I stood still with my eyes closed.

My reverie was finally broken by the familiar sound of a bellowing Irish accent. This dampened my spirits a little, for the voices reminded me of the hollows of the *Havring*.

I began to say *Aleinu*. When I came to the words "*Sheheim mishtachavim lehevel varik umispalalim el ail lo yoshia*" (For they bow to vanity and emptiness and pray to a god which helps not), I opened my eyes and spat towards the open door.

Matthews' three employees were standing there watching me. As I spat, one of them jumped away from me in fright. He looked as though he'd seen the devil. I finished *Aleinu* and walked to the door.

"Now I ask myself, is that any way to greet another man? If you weren't so big, I'd make you rub that spittle over my shoes and polish them until you could see your face in them."

The man who spoke was short and stocky, with a reddish complexion. He looked more than ready to enter into a fight with me.

"Good evening, gentlemen. Whom do I have the pleasure of addressing?" I asked.

"Gentlemen we ain't, sir, but we'll tell you who we

are nonetheless," he answered, apparently placated by my friendly tone. "My name's Tim Darcy, this here is James Masters, and standing behind us both is young Paul Coulhoun. We work for Matthews. And you, sir? Do you have a name?"

"I'm Moses Lazar, named after my grandfather before me." I shook hands with Darcy and Masters. Coulhoun, uncertain whether shaking hands with me might bring him into contact with the satan, remained at a distance.

"You must be the man that Matthews brought down to make us toe the line," said Masters. "You never know what kind of trick he'll pull on poor fellows like us. But I'll tell you this, me lads, just take a look at the size of this fellow. He might do the trick. Take a roll of tobacco?" he asked, offering the contents of a pouch which he pulled from his jacket.

"I don't smoke tobacco."

"What about a shot of the finest rum?" asked Masters, passing a small bottle in front of my face.

"I'm not a drinking man," I answered.

"Then what type of man are you?" he asked.

"A man that needs no vices or spirits to live by," I proudly announced.

"You sound like a priest at the pulpit," said Coulhoun, who remained firmly placed behind Darcy and Masters.

"I'm no priest. I'm of Jewish blood."

"Ha!" laughed Darcy. "One of God's chosen souls. Have you come bearing us miracles, Jew Lazar? Even were you to split the seas all the way back to England, Her Majesty's men would find a way to bring them together over us. And though you Jews wandered in the desert for forty years, that was nothing compared to our sorrowful situation, for we've been thrown into the largest desert that God ever created and it's surrounded by nothing but water."

"Looks as though this land has got the better of you, Mr. Darcy. Although I must say, sir, that you speak like an educated man."

"Educated?" he scoffed. "The only education I ever got was how to steal, and you can see that I didn't come out of that school with too many honors. Are you going to invite us in, Lazar, or do we have to stand out here in the cold?"

He pushed his way past me without waiting for the invitation he had requested. The others followed. They made their way towards the low bench and sat down comfortably as if they'd done so hundreds of times before.

"Gentlemen, I must apologize that I have nothing to offer you. You are my first guests, but I am more a stranger to this room than you are."

"Why should you be offering us anything?" asked Masters, a look of surprise on his face.

"One must treat guests with honor," I answered.

The three men laughed. "The voyage didn't teach you much about your newfound position in life, did it, Moses Lazar?" said Masters. "Let me explain to you all you need to know about hospitality. First, you're not your own master, you own nothing. Consider yourself at the bottom rung of a long ladder. Working for Matthews is the way we serve our fixed terms of punishment. The rest of the men coming off ships are sent to work cutting roads or digging tunnels, putting up buildings and the like. We're what you call 'assigned men.' The government has lent us out to Matthews, and he's put us to work. He has to feed and clothe us, and we're his to do with what he will."

"Matthews seems a decent sort of man," I said. The three men nodded in agreement.

"He's decent as far as landowners go," said Darcy. "I've worked for two before him. They were merciless. We'd be beaten at every opportunity. Matthews doesn't treat us badly. He bribes us with drink, knowing we like more than the odd drop. He drives us hard by day, although we never see him at night, when he's mostly as drunk as we."

"What work do you do?" I asked.

"Either finishing off the fence to the penning yard or shepherding around the hills," answered Masters.

"What's so hard in putting up a fence or chasing sheep?" I asked.

"There's no complaining about the fence. We don't mind that. Matthews keeps an eye on us all day. He never lets up and we go slow to spite him. But if we ever rub him the wrong way he sends us out with the sheep. You see, the pasture grounds aren't as green as other places. The eucalyptus trees soak up all the moisture in the ground. So we need to walk miles just to find the sheep something decent to eat. Matthews has a few hundred head of sheep, and there's nothing harder than chasing after them all day. If you lose one you spend the night out until you find it. But worse than that, we're not armed, and the blacks, aboriginals as we call them here, come and poach the sheep. It's nothing but good fortune that they haven't killed one of us yet."

"And you may as well know it," continued Darcy, "Matthews gives us only one day's rations, so there's no point in trying to escape. Even if we were to try, it wouldn't do us any good because there's nowhere to escape to. Young Coulhoun here was out three days until we found him, half-starved."

I looked at Coulhoun who had swigged consistently from his bottle of spirits since walking into my room. He seemed oblivious to all that was being said.

"Matthews has promised me good conditions if I work hard," I said.

"Has he now?" said Darcy, with a glitter of suspicion in his eye. "Then let me tell you what you'll be working for. I've never heard of it happening before, but if a man behaves better than the governor's own children, he might be granted an absolute pardon. That means a man is given his rights as a free person again and put on a boat back to England. Like I said, it is rare, and even if Matthews has the word in the right person's ear, it wouldn't guarantee a free ticket past the front gate.

"The next step on the ladder is what they call a conditional pardon. You're a free man in the colony.

Open up your own business if it pleases you. The only restriction is that you can't go back to England.

"And finally we have the ticket-of-leave system, where you're free from government work, but your ticket needs renewing every year. It's a tender freedom though, for you might look the wrong way at a man of rank and the ticket will be taken off you. That's life in Australia, Mr. Lazar. Do you like what you hear?"

"One can't give up hope when there's a chance of seeing one's family again."

"Just don't be the fool to work like a slave for Matthews," whispered Coulhoun, who understood more than I had guessed, despite his drunkenness. The other two men nodded in their agreement.

The three got up to leave. Coulhoun held onto Masters as he staggered through the open door and passed over the threshold. Darcy pulled an undershirt out of his coat pocket and slipped a needle from out of his shoe. A large carving knife was wrapped in the shirt.

"I overheard you asking for these. Take it as a gesture of goodwill between us, Moses Lazar." He didn't give me a chance to thank him. He turned and walked away from my room with the other two. After a few paces I heard them stop. It was Darcy who spoke out of the darkness.

"We'll be seeing you in the morning, Moses Lazar. Whatever it was that Matthews might have promised you, just remember that you're of a different class now. You're a convict sent to serve out a sentence. He could change his mind when he's finished with you and nobody in this entire colony, from the governor down, could care less."

With those parting words, they walked into the night. I mused over the conversation for a while, struck by the strange fact that he must have been hiding close by as I drove up with Matthews.

Meanwhile, my mind was set on other matters. I had things to do before morning. I stepped outside and boiled some water. When it was hot I placed the knife Darcy had given me into it and then ran it under some cold water.

I lay down on the hard bed thinking about my first day in Australia. My thoughts turned to my family, and I promised myself that there wasn't a sacrifice I wouldn't make to see them again. I lay on the bed, exhausted, and it wasn't long after saying *Shema* that I fell into a deep sleep.

Chapter 4

Excepting Sundays, work on Matthews' property began soon after daybreak. I started working on a Tuesday, and for three days helped Masters and Darcy with the fences. They were good men to work with, although they insisted on working slowly. My presence must have encouraged them somewhat, for although at first they teased me for putting all my energy into "nothing of consequence," the longer we worked together and the more they heard me speak of my hope and goal of a reunion with my family, the more they became infected by my spirit. Matthews was obviously satisfied and soon after my arrival refrained from his habit of hovering over us like the flies that never gave us a moment's rest.

Friday morning I spoke to Matthews about his promise not to force me to work on Shabbos. He hadn't forgotten, and he kept his word as an honest man. As agreed, I would be responsible for taking the sheep out to pasture on Sunday, when the other men had their day of rest. This particularly pleased Matthews, because before my arrival the sheep never went to pasture on Sundays. I happily accepted, satisfied that I would be able to spend a Shabbos as a Jew should. Masters and Darcy thought I was mad to take Saturday off. The Lord's day of rest didn't come twice a week, they laughed. They were curious as to how I would spend my time, and when I explained to them that I'd refrain from many types of work to fulfill God's commandment, they thought it all very amusing and had a hearty laugh about "Jew Lazar's Sabbath."

Friday morning, not long after we'd begun our daily work, Matthews approached us. "Gentlemen," he said, addressing Masters, Darcy, and Coulhoun. "You are all well aware that once in two weeks we put some meat over the fire. How'd you all like a piece of mutton slaughtered as only Moses Lazar knows how?"

"As long as it's mutton I don't mind who does the killing," said Coulhoun.

"Come then. Let us see how our friend Lazar sheds a little blood."

We made our way to the back of the kitchen, where a sheep had been readied for slaughter.

It is hard to describe the proceedings without mentioning my excitement. Matthews was making good on all his promises. After working with Darcy and Masters for only three days and being told of the hell that some men in the colony were living through, I could only be thankful that in comparison I was living in a veritable paradise.

I thanked Hashem that I had heeded the advice of my father so many years ago, when he had insisted upon my learning the laws and practice of *shechitah*. I took the knife Darcy had given me and sharpened it on the whetting stone. The knife wasn't smooth, and the entire procedure took much time. Matthews' men thought this a matter of hilarity.

"By the time you finish sharpening the edge of that knife, good Jew Lazar, the sheep will have died of old age. Why not take it out of its misery and knock it over the head with a rock?"

Goyim they might have been, but I lost no opportunity in telling them of Hashem's kindness to animals. I tried to explain that Hashem had placed animals like sheep on this earth for our use, but that didn't mean we were to abuse His kindness. The sheep had to be slaughtered in the proper manner. This only brought a few ironic jeers and laughter from the men. Matthews, I must say, never once laughed, which I thought rather out of character.

By the time the knife was sharpened, they knew exactly what I was about to do. Matthews and his men stood around me like children totally mesmerized by some wonderful tale. I held the sheep across my knees, and as I made the *brachah* before *shechitah*, all that could be heard was the wind rustling through the trees and tall grass.

After the deed was done, I cut off a portion for

myself and soaked and salted it as *halachah* demanded as the others looked on. Finally, I roasted it on a spit that I had *kashered*.

That Shabbos, I ate the biggest portion of mutton I had ever enjoyed. I cut it with the knife that I'd *kashered*, ate the loaves of fresh bread that Matthews' cook had baked under my supervision, and drank my cup of rum. I ate some fresh fruits to finish off the repast.

Earlier that day I had asked if anyone possessed a copy of the Old Testament. The only Bible on the farm was a New Testament that belonged to the cook. "A bible's a bible if you want my opinion," said Coulhoun. I promised myself that when I got to Melbourne I'd get myself one.

I remember sleeping most of the day, as the weather wasn't fine enough for anything else. I did venture out once. All to be seen was tall grass and eucalyptus trees, as far as the eye could discern.

The next day I took the sheep out on the run for the first time. I pocketed a loaf of bread and some of the mutton I'd cooked, and Matthews added a large shot of rum. He pointed me in the direction he thought I'd find the most success and left me to it.

The work was difficult, and I hardly found a minute to rest. Keeping hundreds of sheep tightly grouped was more difficult than I had imagined. By mid-morning, I was exhausted, by lunch, unable to stand. It had been less than a week since I'd left the *Havring*, and my strength had not yet returned. After five hours I staggered in through the property gates. Darcy, Masters, and Coulhoun came to my aid. They penned the sheep in while I half walked, half dragged myself into my room. I fell onto the bed and slept soundly until the next morning.

This was the pattern my work took over the next three weeks—working on the fences during the week and taking the sheep out to pasture on Sundays.

Once my strength returned, Sundays became more bearable. On Saturday nights I would lie awake thinking about our forefather Yaakov tending sheep. I pictured the paths they had taken through the ancient hills. Though I was in a land far, far away, the thought gave me a measure of comfort.

One Sunday about a month after my arrival, as I stood alone in the hills, I noticed several of the herd take fright at a movement coming from the thick scrub in the bush on my left. At first I didn't pay attention, as such occurrences were frequent. I was interested only in pushing the herd forward to better pasture further ahead.

Fifty paces on, the sheep, frightened once again, bolted in panic. I walked over to the bush to investigate, searching for signs of the disturbance, but my bush sense wasn't sufficiently developed for me to detect anything out of the ordinary. I was suspicious nonetheless and kept a sharp eye open.

Then I saw them—two very black, scantily attired figures hiding behind the scrub. They didn't seem surprised that I'd seen them and made no attempt to flee. From where I stood, maybe one hundred yards away, I could make out the outline of a sheep lying on its side next to one of them. The one on the left stood up. He was tall and sinewy, with an extremely muscular chest. He wore a loincloth and had wrapped a blanket around himself for warmth. Both he and the other fellow, who was as tall and as well-proportioned, carried long spears.

When it became apparent to them that I was not going to run away in fright, they shook their spears at me angrily. I had no idea what to do. Certainly the wisest course of action would have been to flee, but that would have meant leaving the sheep unattended. In truth, the reason I stood my ground was because I wasn't really aware of the danger I faced. They were close but not close enough for me to feel threatened. Were they to advance on me, I told myself, I could flee. So I remained standing where I was, listening to them chatter away in their strange tongue.

One of them placed the end of his spear into a long, tube-like piece of bark. He drew his arm back and took careful aim. Alarmed, I turned to flee, only partly aware of the dangerous missile headed in my direction. It passed not half a foot from my left side and quivered into a nearby tree.

There was no need debating as to my next course of action. I ran as fast as my legs would carry me, terrified that the powerful throw of the black men might reach me no matter how far I ran.

I hadn't gone twenty paces when another spear hit a tree just to the right of my head. I was overcome by fear and anger. Fear, because my life was in danger of being taken from me by these two primitive blacks, and anger, because I wasn't ready to die. I had much to do before passing on to the next world. I took a deep breath and kept running. Yet what use was there running? They would catch me if that's what they wanted. I prayed to Hashem, begging Him for mercy.

I turned to see my attackers. They were closer than before, maybe sixty paces away, looking like wild beasts closing in on their prey. One of them then took a long, thick stick out of the cloth that covered his waist and drew it behind his head. Just as he prepared to hurtle it towards me, a shot rang out from the bush. The black fellows looked in that direction and without a sound bolted away in the opposite direction.

Out of the bush rode Matthews atop a dark brown horse. He rode past me in pursuit of the black men, but returned moments later.

"Scoundrels!" he cursed, as he jumped off his horse. "Did they kill any sheep?" I told him of the one I'd seen lying by their side. "That's the first time they've actually attacked. That stick they wield is deadly. I've seen one of them kill a kangaroo at two hundred paces."

"God caused you to appear at a fortunate time, Mr. Matthews."

"Yes," he answered. "I hadn't planned on coming out. Something made me do it though. You might call it the hand of God."

"There's no doubt in my mind that it was He that brought you to my rescue. It seems He has more for me to do in this world than die at the hands of some savages." This evoked a laugh from Matthews.

"What's that?" he said, pointing to the spear sticking into the tree trunk. I told him of the two spears that were intended for me. "They were either toying with you or you're just plain lucky. No matter, Lazar, the important thing is that you're alive to see another day. Let's go, man. We've hundreds of sheep to round up. Let's bring them back in. Those black fellows might come back with ten or more of their kind and not even this shooting piece could ward them all off."

On the way back to the station Matthews told me of his plight with the black aboriginals. On the one hand, he was furious with their persistent threats to his men, but at the same time, he showed an unusual understanding for them. The aboriginals hated white men, he told me, because since the founding of the land by the English, they had been dispossessed wherever the white man roamed.

We rode on in silence, and then he abruptly said, "I'm riding into Melbourne today. I'll be there until tomorrow night. Whilst there I'll speak to a couple of men who have experience in the bush. I may employ a few more hands to help me protect the herd."

I reminded Matthews that I was intensely eager to speak to the man Hart and indeed wanted to strike up bonds between myself and other Jews here in Australia. Matthews agreed to my accompanying him without hesitation, only asking that I refrain from telling the other men why I was being allowed such liberty.

Chapter 5

The Melbourne I live in today bears little resemblance to the Melbourne I recall in 1849. Then it was nothing more than a small settlement called the Port Philip District. Many of its commercial affairs were run from Sydney. The town center was a crisscross of stores opening onto wide, unpaved streets. The atmosphere was pastoral. Drink, and there was always plenty of it, was usually the instigator to the rowdier side of life. Possibly the remoteness of the settlement and the boredom of life here caused the excess of drunkenness I witnessed.

I wasn't exactly shown around the town like an honored guest. The observations I made depended upon the speed of the horses running in front of us.

Matthews stopped on what he claimed to be the most famous landmark in the colony, Cashmore's Corner. It was distinguished because there stood a building two stories in height, the highest building in the colony at the time. He left the carriage outside, crossed to the other side of the road, and entered a large store called London Mart, owned by the Jews Harris and Marks. When he returned he told me that I would probably find Asher Hart at the newly constructed synagogue.

He guided his horses towards the synagogue, and left me there, telling me to meet him on Cashmore's Corner the following day at four in the afternoon.

The synagogue was situated on the top of a small hill surrounded by a wooden picket fence. I opened the gate and walked up the unattended path. The building was square in shape and had five high windows which were rounded at the top. I tapped lightly on one of the windows to draw the attention of the only man inside. He motioned me round the side of the building and met me at the door.

I was finally face to face with a Jew, a compatriot. I was so excited I could hardly utter anything coherent. I recall him asking if there was anything the matter. Finally, after what must have seemed forever, I burst out with, "Shalom Aleichem!"

His eyebrows rose. "Aleichem Shalom." I firmly gripped his hand and shook it until he was forced to wrench it out of mine.

"Are you Asher Hyman Hart?" I nervously asked.

"I am," he replied.

"My name is Lazar. Moses Lazar. I am presently under the employ of George Matthews. I arrived a month ago on the *Havring*."

"Are you a free settler or was your passage spent under deck?" he asked.

"The latter, I'm afraid to say."

"Never mind, Moses. If you're of Jewish blood you're most certainly welcome here."

"Would I be right in assuming that the congregation will soon be praying the afternoon prayers?" I asked.

Hart hesitated momentarily, surprised by the question. "Not quite!" came his reply. "We don't hold regular services." He must have detected the look of disappointment on my face. He cordially invited me inside, and when I asked to see the *aron hakodesh*, he led me to it, opened it, and took out the one Torah there. I touched the finely embroidered cover and brought my lips to it. All the emotion I had suppressed for so long seemed to explode within me, overwhelming me, reducing me to tears. I prayed Minchah alone, as I had for nearly half a year, while Hart watched in obvious sympathy. At last I was praying in Hashem's house.

When I had finished, Hart invited me into the small office at the back of the synagogue. There I told him my story. The more I told him, the more interest he showed. When I was done he grabbed my hand and shook it as fervently as I had shaken his only an hour earlier.

"Moses Lazar, you are sent from heaven. You can read Hebrew, read from the Torah, and perform *shechitah*. You are precisely the type of man we are looking for. Are you a *mohel*?" I answered in the negative. The glow in his eyes dimmed a bit. "Can you sing *chazanus*?" Again I replied in the negative. His face fell somewhat. "We are in need of a man who can perform these functions."

"I'd be of no use to you anyway, Mr. Hart. I still hold the unfortunate title of 'government man.' "

"You're not like other convicts," he said. "It's not fitting for one of your fine character to have been brought down so low in life."

"*HaKadosh Baruch Hu* has His ways," I uttered. "I've been sent out here at His will. I have faith that all will turn out for the best."

"It's a brave man who speaks words like those," Hart said. After a pause, he continued. "I've heard of this George Matthews. He's a fair man and treats his men well. Quite an anomaly in these parts. I will speak to him about your position."

We then discussed my dream of bringing my family out to Australia. Hart seemed optimistic and suggested that should I work hard and honestly it was a real possibility. Finally, I broached another important issue: my intention of obtaining mezuzahs, a Chumash, and a siddur. Hart walked over to a locked cabinet, took out all the precious items I'd requested, and smilingly presented them to me. In addition, he gave me a small volume of *mishnayos*. I felt most grateful to him and wished I could have remunerated him for his kindness. As it was I hadn't even a penny to put into the *tzedakah* box.

I spent most of my free time that day with Hart, and

to his honor and good name I will say he was a gentleman in the true sense of the word, acting neither officiously nor pretentiously in his dealings with me. Later that night he introduced me to two men, Samuel Isaacs and Walter Lindenthal, who were in charge of many communal services.

Melbourne's total Jewish population only consisted of some two hundred souls, they told me. For the most part the congregation wasn't wealthy, although there were a few notables among them.

I was given board that night at Hart's fine and stately residence. We sat late into the night discussing the settlement and the opportunities that might await me should I successfully petition the governor for freedom.

I saw immediately that among the Jews of the colony only a handful were fully observant of the faith that lay at the very core of my existence. Their distance from the bubbling, teeming life of Jewish England was cause enough for many to lose contact with the very fundamentals of their Yiddishkeit. Not until early 1849, for example, did the congregation appoint a *shochet*. Until then, Jews wishing to purchase kosher meat had an obvious difficulty. Such matters are taken for granted by established communities.

But the difficulty lay deeper then with the lack of communual organizations and services. Today I see snowballing assimilation even though the Melbourne of 1879 can boast of almost everything a Jew needs: a shul, *sifrei Torah, mohel,* and *shochet*. These basics can't ensure that the community will remain faithful to the tenets of Torah.

The *yetzer hara* that tempts men into forgetting who they are hovers over the skies in Melbourne like a dark rain cloud. Some men get soaked to the skin; others get slightly wet, but the taste of temptation is enough to find them looking forward to the next downpour. And so many are lost.

Such were the initial impressions I gained during my first visit to Melbourne. I fell asleep that night pondering the consequences of bringing my family out to Australia. A premature fear obviously: I was a long way from that joyous reunion. And yet I wondered, if I were to do so, would I have a difficult time educating them in the proper Jewish manner? Two hundred Jews amidst a sea of *goyim* is formula enough for fear. But my days in the colony were few and I had much to do before I could hope to see my dreams come to fruition. What else was there for me to do other than continue on my way, pray, and maintain faith in Hashem?

The following day I awoke early and prayed alone in the synagogue. I had until four to meet Matthews and could think of no better way to spend some of my time than by doing a little learning. The library in the synagogue was small, but sufficed. I admit I was no great scholar and to learn alone took enormous effort. For four hours I sat with an open Chumash in front of me.

Since being caught with the flour in my pocket so many months before, my mind had been in constant turmoil. I had thoughts only of my family's plight and my own situation. It was as though I had a ball and chain attached around my neck. Somehow, the learning loosened the chain. I felt a clarity and peace of mind that I had rarely achieved in life. I read the *parshah* of *Shemos*. Reading of the bondage our forefathers had to endure before their emancipation from Egypt brought me hope. If Hashem could take all of *bnei Yisrael* out of Egypt, surely He could help me survive my imprisonment and take me out of bondage. All that was required of me was faith and the will to survive.

At noon I made my way down to Cashmore's Corner, meaning to enter the London Mart. I crossed the road and looked into the shop windows. The items on display were as varied as the shapes of snow. They sold everything a man's heart could desire. I was eyeing the items, some of which my wife would have been delighted to own, when I caught a glimpse of Matthews in the reflection of the plateglass window. He hadn't seen me. After making certain it was he, I started walking towards him, when I heard a yell from across the street.

"You fiend!" came the shout. "Fiend, I say!" Matthews turned around to face his caller. I noticed a pale and pained look come over his face. The man motioned to him but did not approach. Matthews seemed frozen and stared as though he'd seen an apparition.

I looked closely at the man. He was about fifty years of age, but his rounded, hunched back gave him the appearance of being much older. His clothes were badly cut. He sported a long beard and wore a hat on his head. There was something coarse in the voice which had yelled, but the features of his face were gentle and kind. Yet there was nothing highly unusual about him. What was it about the man that frightened Matthews so?

Curious to see what would ensue, I kept a safe distance from Matthews and crossed the road behind him. Matthews came within touching distance of the man, who eyed him carefully from head to toe. Then he stared deep into Matthews' eyes. Matthews looked away in shame. The man spat at Matthews' feet, turned on his heels, and quite suddenly disappeared into a small crowd of shoppers on Cashmore's Corner.

Matthews stood in his tracks. He looked dejected and shocked. He stood where he was for five minutes, not moving an inch, rigid as a statue.

I mingled with the crowd on Cashmore's Corner, hoping to catch sight of the man who'd had such a stunning effect on my employer, yet no matter where I looked I couldn't find him.

Returning, I found Matthews walking slowly down the middle of the road, his head bent low, his hands in his pockets. I thought it best not to pursue him. He probably wouldn't have appreciated my arrival in the mood he was in.

The episode was mysterious indeed. When I met Matthews at the appointed hour, he was in a state of indolence and indifference. I assumed that he hadn't employed more men because we drove out alone. I deemed it wise to maintain a silence on our journey, and less than two hours later we rode over the small ridge which led down into his property. Without a word I alighted from the carriage and walked to my room, eager to put up my mezuzah and feel that I was finally creating the beginnings of a Jewish home.

That night I slept restlessly. Matthews' mysterious meeting with the stranger kept my mind busily at work. The stranger's face haunted me. I had never seen him before, but the gentle look in his eyes had a ring of familiarity to it, far too familiar for me to rest peacefully.

Chapter 6

Many weeks passed before Matthews returned to his former self. He was severely agitated and rarely bothered with the day-to-day details of his property. The other men had no inclination to see to anything they weren't asked to do, and so I found myself carrying the responsibility which should have lain exclusively with Matthews. The meeting with the stranger had taken its toll, and he kept to his rooms and thoroughly soaked himself in spirits. He looked and reeked as if he'd sat in a bath of rum for a month. When our paths did cross, he showed surprise at my initiative, and, depressed as he may have been, I knew that his appraisal of me rose considerably as a result.

Then an incident took place which brought our lives closer together. As I said, Matthews rarely bothered with us in those days. If, however, he did decide to check on us and found us not working to his liking, he exploded into a fury. His bad temper and moody disposition bred constant fear in us. If ever we spied him coming to check our work, we'd put our backs into it for fear of sparking his anger.

The fences were completed three weeks after our return from Melbourne, and two men were sent out together daily to graze the sheep. The property was running smoothly, but in those days the more successful it became, the more Matthews' anger and depression intensified.

Darcy and I had been working hard and silently all morning building a new fodder room. At eleven o'clock we took our first break and, deservedly, sat down on some hay to rest. I pulled out my small book of *mishnayos* while Darcy rolled himself some tobacco. Out of nowhere, as if he'd been waiting for the opportunity to pounce on us all morning, Matthews stood above us both.

"What the devil! Is this the way you work for a man, by resting away the morning hours!?" Without giving us the opportunity to respond to his accusations, he was at us again, cursing our very existence. Only a day earlier Darcy had spoken out about Matthews' temperament, saying he'd just about had enough. Darcy could be dangerous because he had no control over his anger. Once he resorted to using his fists, he'd continue punching and kicking until he either beat the other man senseless or was felled himself. He was a ball of Irish fury.

Darcy sat smoking his tobacco, giving the impression that he wasn't perturbed by Matthews' anger. Yet, knowing Darcy as I did, I could sense that there wouldn't be much more pushing him before he'd lose his head.

"The only hard work the lot of you do is lift your food bowls to your mouths!" screamed Matthews, becoming more deranged. "Speak up!" he said, glaring at us wildly. "Your excuses better be worthy of listening to or I'll turn you over to the governor."

I told him how hard we'd worked and that he had nothing to hold against us. On the contrary, he should be happy with the hours we'd put into the work. Every curse or slander he flung our way I countered as gently as I could. My first concern was for Matthews. I was aware of his distress and realized that he had utilized this moment to release his tension. I only wished to protect him from Darcy.

My second concern was for Darcy himself. I owed him no favors, but he was a simple man, worth keeping out of trouble if for no other reason than I had taken a liking to him, even if he was a brash, tobacco-smoking Irishman.

Again Matthews cursed, this time venting his anger in Darcy's direction. He must have used all the expletives that existed in the English language. Though I was on my guard, when Darcy did pounce it took me unawares. His open hands groped and found Matthews' throat. Matthews seemed strangely calm as Darcy's grip tightened, as though he had taunted the man in the hope he'd be killed.

I grabbed Darcy's arms and pressed my thumbs deep into his wrists. He let go, and went to attack again. I caught him, gripped him in a bear hug, and held on while he flailed and kicked the air like a captive beast.

It took quite some time to calm him down, and when he was calm I released him. He fell to the ground breathing heavily, his head turned away from my gaze. Matthews lay prone on the ground clutching his wounded throat. I helped him to his feet, took him to his rooms, and lay him on his bed. At the door I asked whether there was anything he needed. His answer was short and disturbing.

"For Darcy to have more luck next time."

On my way back to the fodder room, the episode, and Matthews' words, ran through my head. Matthews wanted Darcy to murder him? I found that hard to believe. If the man was so intent upon ending his life, why entice another to do the job for him? Besides, Matthews must have realized that I would have come between them. Perhaps that's what he had relied on?

I found Darcy as I had left him, lying on the floor of the fodder room. His breathing was back to normal and he was relatively calm and thoughtful, the full weight of his folly having caught up with him.

"When's he riding out to bring the governor's men in?"

"Who's to say he will?" I answered.

"Who's to say I care?" he ventured.

"Come, Tim Darcy. Are you trying to tell Moses

Lazar that you'd prefer the insides of jail? I say you care! I think you might still find yourself employed once you lift yourself off the ground. I don't think he has the slightest intention of firing you."

Nor did he! Matthews remained locked in his room married to his rum, and when he did emerge from his drunkenness, three days later, not as heavily depressed as when he first entered it, he found his property as he'd left it: in full working order.

In England, Tishah B'Av is the longest fast day of the year, while in Australia it is the shortest. My first Tishah B'Av was spent working as usual. I did much thinking that day. How I wished that Her Majesty had sent me to work as a slave in Jerusalem. At least there my burden could have been endured with the knowledge that I dwelt where the *shechinah* had rested. It was from that first Tishah B'Av that I became obsessed with the idea of Jerusalem being the most fitting place for Jews to settle. I had never heard of anyone traveling there to live, but the idea rooted itself firmly in my mind then, and years later I still dream of living in the land of our forefathers. Ever since my banishment from England I have realized that we are strangers in every country in which we settle.

Such thoughts are most often expressed by those who haven't seen success in life. They might not have Jerusalem in mind, but when they have lost all hope they turn their minds to dreams of a life richer in quality. Today I am wealthier than most men in this colony and have seen more gold coins than I can remember, and yet I realize that we Jews don't belong in the Englands and Australias of this world. We belong in one place only—the place we point our bodies and minds to when we pray to the Almighty every day.

It was early September and the spring weather had arrived. The beginning of the Australian spring comes just when England is preparing for the cold of winter, and this has always been rather startling to me. I had been working for Matthews for three months. The high holidays were a matter of days away, and I hoped to spend them in Melbourne. I was to travel there and back four times, for Rosh Hashanah, Yom Kippur, and the first and last days of Sukkos. Matthews had begun to rely on me and affably acceded to my requests. A day before Rosh Hashanah he called me to his rooms. He was sitting at his writing desk looking over a document.

"How often do you write to your family?" he asked me.

"Once a week," I answered.

"And they have written to you?"

"I've only received one letter."

"What is their position?"

"They are living through hard times. They are poor but healthy."

Quite matter-of-factly he handed me the documents he'd been handling. "This shall be sent out on the next ship to England. With your approval, of course."

I looked at the documents. One document was a

money transfer to be forwarded to my wife, the other, a notice to a migrant shipping firm in London requesting the purchase of three tickets on the passage to Melbourne.

"You've proved yourself to me in more ways than one, Moses Lazar. In more ways than you'll ever know. Take it as a sign of appreciation. If my calculations are correct, you can expect to see your family by next April. Meanwhile, you'll continue working for me. I'd like you to stay on after they come and help me run the property."

"Of course," I stammered. I thanked Matthews a thousand times, and he, seeing the tears welling in my eyes, hit me hard on the shoulder in a brotherly type of way.

"You'll have to travel alone tomorrow. By foot I'm afraid. It won't take you longer than four hours. You can leave at noon. I'll expect to see you back early Sunday morning. Leave these documents with Hart. He'll make certain that they are forwarded at the first opportunity. You looked a bit dazed, Moses. Come man! There's much to do until you leave."

I was so numb that it took me some time to return to a rational state. That I was to see my wife and children so soon after leaving them was nothing less than a miracle. We were going to start our lives over. There'd be new opportunities, a chance to succeed. "*Modeh ani lefanechah*," I shouted aloud, "*Melech chai vekayam!*"

Now that I could actually envisage in real terms

being reunited with my wife, I was able to be more objective in my view of England and Australia. I had lived my life in the slum of London and found it hard to recall anything other than the filth, the smell, the overcrowding, the disease which resulted from all three, the lack of opportunity, the utter hopelessness of each and every hour of the day. Australia, on the other hand, offered the openness of its spaces. The climate wasn't harsh, the opportunities were numerous, and, moreover, there was a sense of challenge, an aura of hope which hung over the people I'd met. Australia was where the chances lay. Once my family arrived, we'd set our sights at working towards a comfortable life here. Such was my happiness on the eve of Rosh Hashanah, 1849.

Chapter 7

I admit that back then I was a naive young man, naive enough to suppose that all the two hundred Jewish souls of the colony would attend the New Year services. It came as a shock when I learned that the majority didn't attend. Since then I have lost my naiveté, and yet, somehow I've never grown accustomed to the unfortunate reality. Little has altered in this respect since my first year in Melbourne. Today, Melbourne's population has increased both in size and influence, but the number count at synagogue come festival time sadly remains terribly small.

I entered Melbourne on Erev Rosh Hashanah, 1849, in a dream world. My journey was accompanied by intermittent rain and warm bouts of sunshine, and even if I did walk into town rather damp, I was not in the least disheartened. There was no happier man to be found in the town.

Asher Hart was thrilled by the mail I brought him. He shook my hand vigorously and promised to send out the invitations to my family at the first opportunity. He was pleased to see me and, as he and his family had done on my first visit, went out of his way to make my stay as comfortable as possible.

Hart kept a traditional home, and though he lacked much in knowledge of Yiddishkeit, he was an unselfish and pious man. He and his family accompanied me to the synagogue by foot, and his excitement and pride that the New Year prayers were to be heard in the newly dedicated synagogue were all too obvious. To me he represented a most important element in the community. Without his efforts in building the synagogue and in seeking out the right people to serve as the spiritual leaders of the community, Melbourne Jewry, weak as it is, might have taken even longer to consolidate itself, and many more might have found themselves totally swept away into the ominous maelstrom of assimilation.

Once inside the synagogue I took a *machzor*, moved to a back corner, and waited for Minchah to begin. Worshipers began to occupy seats. I could sense in the worshipers the same feeling of pride that emanated from Hart. The moment was truly special.

We began to daven. For a year I had been forced to daven alone, and no matter how much *kavanah* one puts into prayer, nothing compares to davening with a minyan. I was particularly moved when the *chazan*, John Henry Anderson of Tasmania, broke into the melodies I remembered from England.

There is one thing in particular which made my first Rosh Hashanah in Australia significant. There were only a few among us who were, for want of a better phrase, conscientious in prayer. On many an occasion I, or one of them, would lift our heads up from our *machzorim* and catch a glance of those who I will term the "not-so-conscientious." Their looks have remained engraved in my mind's eye, from where they refuse to be erased. I read their looks with sad clarity: they were looks of pity. They said to men like me:

"You poor souls. Don't you realize that we are in Australia now where our ties to the Almighty have faded? The unfathomable distance between us and Europe has cut us off and limited our ties to the old world. Jews we may be, but there's a limit to the length we must go to internalize the fact."

I have since conversed with hundreds of these types of Jews and become melancholy at their attitude. Judaism to them is little more than an identity from which bits and pieces are drawn at the whim of the user. These lost souls believe that Judaism cannot find its place in the remoteness of Australia. Like poor children gazing in at a bakery, they are barred from the delights within, unable to savor the wonder of Torah and Yiddishkeit.

The services came to an end. All the congregants stood around talking. The evening was warm and no one was in a hurry to go home. Many of the men were free immigrants, and I was curious to know how they compared England with Australia. Hardships may have taken their toll on some of them, but, I concluded, most were happy with what these strange shores had offered them.

Hart beckoned to me from across the synagogue and soon we were walking in step, his family a few paces behind, back to his residence. He took a different route this time which, to his dismay, took us past a rowdy drinking establishment. Outside, men were loitering around, drunk or nearly drunk. Hart and I fell alongside his family, flanking them, he near the road and I on the side closest the public bar, ignoring the coarse remarks so similar to the sounds of the *Havring* which I thought I'd succeeded in putting out of my mind.

As I was on the side closest to the building, I didn't notice a man approach Hart from the other side. But I heard his voice.

"Such a lovely night to be out walking. Too lovely a night for trouble, wouldn't you say?"

I instantly recognized the voice, and rather than confront it, ushered the women and children along at a quicker pace. The brute then addressed Hart deprecatingly.

"Does the gentleman happen to have a few shillings to put to the worthy cause of drink?"

"I've nothing for the likes of you. Now let me pass or I'll call for the law."

Hart's reply played right into the hands of the cunning fiend, who burst into sadistic laughter. The instinct which had kept me alive on the *Havring* told me that Hart had just walked into a fight that couldn't be avoided. The fellow's voice turned threatening.

"The law? I'll carve you into eights before you get the chance, you rich dog."

"And if Jack O'Hearn so much as makes another move he'll have me to reckon with," I countered threateningly.

Not a soul moved and not a sound was heard, even from the drunkards. I hadn't moved from my place, but the women and children, finding the moment convenient, ran ahead with Hart out of danger. The rowdy scum began urging their hero on, hoping he'd fight me for a little entertainment.

I now faced Jack O'Hearn. The only change I could see in him was that Australia had returned him to one of his favorite pastimes—drinking spirits. He was half drunk and, as I had always known him, brimming with malice. When he saw me he seemed slightly ill at ease. His drunkenness wasn't enough to erase the memory of my face and how I had matched him on the passage over.

"Well, if it isn't Jew Lazar dressed up like a nobleman," he bellowed. "Australia's fattened you, Jew. What are you doing out of bondage? Or did you buy your way clear of trouble?"

He was talkative, and only I knew why. He was biding his time. It was usual for O'Hearn to fight first and ask questions later. He knew he'd picked the wrong man to meddle with and was trying to talk his way out of trouble.

"Jack O'Hearn," I said in a quiet but calm voice, "if you think you can give me a hiding in your drunken state, don't forget that you provoked Moses Lazar once before and paid a hefty price. I'm going to walk away from here and you're not going to bother me as I do. We're not walking the streets looking for trouble. We're minding our business and keeping the law."

A large, jeering crowd had gathered around. I think we both realized we'd have to fight each other, because he'd lose face in front of his slovenly peers if he didn't. Shouts of "Come on, Jack, me lad," and "Show him some brawn," were quickly influencing O'Hearn into action. I noticed the cockiness return to his glassy eyes. He looked invincible to all around him.

I was in no mood to fight but saw no other way to rejoin Hart and his family. A fury burned inside me. Did I have to capitulate to the depths of depravity and fight like a drunkard on Rosh Hashanah? I began to walk away.

"Lazar," O'Hearn said confidently, "you're as good as a dead man."

With this he ran towards me in a towering rage. I faced him and stood my ground. Just as he was upon me I crouched, and as he made contact, I lifted him high over my head. He cartwheeled face down onto the road with a terrible thud. The shouts of the crowd turned to hushed surprise. I then fell upon him, placing the full weight of my knees into his back. I lifted his head back with my hands. His eyes were partially open. I leaned over in the dark and whispered quickly in his ear:

"If you're wise, O'Hearn, stay where you are and play like a dead man. Forget about tonight or we'll both live to suffer the consequences."

I got up and walked back a pace or two. Some drunkard cried, "Up with you, O'Hearn!"

O'Hearn, however, didn't move.

"You knocked him out!" cried one of his mates.

"Jack's been bowled over," another laughed.

I saw no need to wait for applause or congratulation and walked down the road to rejoin the Hart family. Nor did I bother to look around once I had rejoined them.

But I knew the chapter hadn't ended with this victory. O'Hearn had been humiliated in front of his own, and when he would come out of his drunken state he'd leave no stone unturned until he found me. And once he did he'd stop at nothing to repay the insult.

I fell into step again with the Hart family. The women were still visibly upset. Hart thanked me for extracting him from a certain beating and promised to bring the matter before the authorities. "Such characters," he said, "shouldn't harass the law-abiding."

As for myself, I tried my best to forget the encounter, and, after the excitement of the meeting had diminished somewhat, I was able to return my mind to where it belonged—to Rosh Hashanah and the importance of *teshuvah*.

Over the next two days we took a circuitous route to the synagogue to avoid confrontation with O'Hearn. Whether or not he was still in the city I'll never know.

We were not harassed any further, and the remainder of the two days of Rosh Hashanah were spent in fervent prayer and a healthy family atmosphere. Indeed, Yom Kippur and Sukkos, too, passed peacefully, and by Simchas Torah I had quite forgotten about the incident.

Jack O'Hearn, however, hadn't.

Between the end of the holidays and April, when my family was due to arrive, life on Matthews' property continued as before. The work was monotonous and the other men became restless. Their complaints began as a trickle but soon came to encompass every moment of their working hours.

If it wasn't the food, living conditions, hours on the job, lack of freedom, or lack of contact with the outside world, they found it expedient to complain about me. They had never accepted the status and recognition that Matthews bestowed upon me. I, using as much insight into the situation as I could muster, worked alongside them as an equal and never took advantage of my position. The three of them began maintaining distance from me when they found out that my family was to be making the voyage out to Australia, patronaged by Matthews himself. Darcy and Masters found this too bitter a pill to swallow. Coulhoun, not gifted with too bright a head, quickly fell into suit with them.

The year 1849 was coming to an end, and Matthews had promised all three men permission to take leave and celebrate New Year's Day in town. They spruced themselves up and looked quite dandy as they left the property. When they returned a few days later, their attitude towards me had hardened. Coulhoun would look at me and whistle in disbelief. Masters and Darcy continued to maintain distance from me, but gave me a newfound respect which rather amused me. Coulhoun later told me it was due to the reputation I'd earned as being the only man alive to put Jack O'Hearn down.

Unfortunately, matters weren't to end there. They may have shown me respect and they may have worked hard, but as time went on I got the distinct impression that there was danger in the air. I took my troubles to Matthews. Perhaps, I told him, O'Hearn, having found out my whereabouts, might try to enter the property to seek his revenge or cause damage to the property itself. If this was the case, I suspected Darcy and Masters would somehow be involved. Matthews asked me how I came to such a deduction. I answered that my experience on the *Havring* had left an indelible mark on me, and it was easy to surmise what course of action a man like O'Hearn would take. I asked Matthews permission to deal with the matter immediately. I suggested that he give the three men the following day off to go into town. He reluctantly agreed.

It was ten o'clock at night. I left Matthews and walked to where Darcy and Masters usually sat talking into the night. When they saw me approach they grew silent.

"Good evening," I said.

"So it is," replied Masters.

I wasted no time coming to the point.

"I suppose you didn't run into Jack O'Hearn while you were in Melbourne?" I asked.

"What's it to you if we did?" snapped Darcy.

"To me? Why, it's nothing to me at all," I answered. "It might be something to you, though." Both their heads lifted when I said this. I stayed silent, waiting for their curiosity to get the better of them.

Darcy was the first to speak. "What could it mean to us?" he asked.

They were sitting on the small porch outside their rooms. I moved towards them and came to within breathing distance of Darcy's face. I spoke in a quiet and threatening voice.

"It means that should Jack O'Hearn or any of his cronies come poking their heads around this property, even for a sniff, I'll break every bone in your body," and, turning to Masters, I emphasized, "and yours!"

They were clearly disturbed by what I said. Masters was apologetic.

"Now, do you think we'd ever do anything to harm you, Moses?"

"Us?" added Darcy.

"I do. Just remember. Every last bone in your bodies!"

Before they had a chance to say anything more I was on my way back to my room, disgusted at the need to speak in such terms to men who understood nothing else, and yet relieved that my message seemed to have been received.

As discussed, Matthews gave them the coming weekend off. As they were making their way off the property, I approached them menacingly. They were clearly agitated.

"Got the day off, have we?" They didn't answer. I must have been standing ten paces from them. I lifted myself to my full height and marched towards them like a storm. One might have heard their bones shake from fear. "Have yourselves a pleasant journey, gentlemen," I said.

When they returned two days later their demeanor had changed completely. Both Darcy and Masters acted as if a great weight had been taken off their shoulders. I told Matthews that if they had been planning anything with anyone in Melbourne, the plan was as good as dead. Men like Darcy and Masters, I told him, turn to jelly when their own skins are at stake.

Chapter 8

I will always cherish the memories of the first *chagim* I spent in Australia. The *sukkah* I helped build outside the synagogue as well as the small *sukkah* I built on Matthews' property taught me that with a little effort and a lot of faith, a man can fulfill the will of the Almighty.

By the time Chanukah arrived, the weather had become increasingly hot, so hot that it was possible to fry an egg on a piece of metal left lying in the sun. I remember seeing Masters do that on more than one occasion. It reminded me of a *mishnah* my father had taught me as a boy. I searched until I located it in the third chapter of Shabbos. Such was my enthusiasm that I learned the entire *mishnayos* of Shabbos.

Little things as seemingly irrelevant as cooking an egg in the sun and being able to find a source for it in the *mishnayos* thrilled me because I wanted to constantly remind myself of the Almighty's presence. Such mind games regularly occupied me. It was a conscious and important effort that saved my spiritual life from total abandonment. The depressing feeling of detachment from Jewish communal life had to be fought alone, and in order to win the battle of loneliness, learning *mishnayos*, sometimes by heart, was a constructive and worthwhile pastime.

Since my first near disastrous encounter with the aboriginals, Matthews' attitude towards them had changed. He came to the astonishing decision that it would be worth his while to befriend them. This, or so I thought when he first outlined his plan to me, would be at great danger to his life and mine. His plan was to journey into the bush to look for them. I thought him mad and bereft of common sense. He, however, insisted that if there was nothing but antagonism between the aboriginals and ourselves, the whole matter would eventually end in tragedy. I admitted, albeit somewhat reluctantly, to the logic behind his reasoning, and agreed to accompany him into the bush on what Darcy called a passage to a quick death. I remember Darcy quite seriously looking Matthews in the eye and asking whether he, Tim Darcy, was expected to mind the property not only after Matthews had passed through the gates of the property, but after he had passed from this world as well.

We left for the bush one hot Sunday morning, planning to return later that day. Matthews was laden with "gifts"—sweetmeats, bright clothing, and an assortment of cheap jewelry. They were to be used, not for barter as I first surmised, but rather as peace offerings.

Once outside the property, Matthews guided his horse through the bush as though he knew precisely where to find the tribe whom we'd skirmished with. After a three hour ride, he got off his horse and bid me to do the same. He untied the parcels of gifts and we proceeded deeper into the bush on foot.

"The bush," as it is fondly known in Australia, is a term given to describe rough, uncivilized land. Australia at the time of my arrival was mostly bush: smooth hills covered in knee-high scrub and grass peppered by the ubiquitous eucalyptus tree. Matthews made his way through the dense undergrowth, I followed closely. It was as if he'd been over this territory hundreds of times before. I was amazed at his bush sense. He seemed as attached to the land as the aboriginals we were looking for.

After walking like this for half a mile he stopped. He then turned to me and pointed between two trees. I could see a tribe of black men, women, and children sitting outside a humpy, which is what we call a tent.

"You can stay here if you like. It might be dangerous," he said.

"I'm a brave man but I won't take any unnecessary risks with my life," I answered. "I'll stand behind you and watch."

"Is this the man who felled the brute O'Hearn?" he laughed.

"It is," I replied. "But there's a major difference. I beat O'Hearn at his own game. Those primitives over there have a set of rules I'm not accustomed to."

"Here I go, then," he said with a laugh.

"Be careful, George," I said. It was the first time I'd ever addressed him by his first name.

He walked forward a few paces and, before the aboriginals spotted him, cried out loudly so they'd hear him. Their first reaction was to look in his direction and take fright. I was certain that the two athletic fellows who'd attacked me months earlier would take their spears and fling them at him. Thankfully, I was wrong. Matthews was too quick for them. They hadn't time to react before he was displaying his wares high above his head. First it was a piece of clothing. Then he put that in his bag and extracted another item. At the same time, ever so slowly, he moved closer to them. It wasn't long before he was no more than twenty feet away. Their curiosity had gotten the better of them, and by the time he'd displayed all his wares three or four times, they were looking quite tame. He took an item of clothing from his bag and threw it towards them. One of the men picked it up. Seeing it was a shirt he put it around his shoulders.

The shirt was now all that covered him. Indeed, none of them there wore anything at all. The two men who'd attacked me were covered, but not with clothes. They wore a type of body paint. I later learned that they made the paint from rocks, leaves, and animals. The colors were stunning in their beauty.

Again Matthews threw an item forward. This time he directed it at our young warriors. They seemed delighted with their prize. Matthews did this a few times. Each time he threw an item, I noticed he directed it towards a member of the tribe whom he supposed might offer resistance to his mission. Now the aboriginals were gesturing towards him. They showed signs of understanding Matthews' intentions and being mesmerized by his performance.

This went on for maybe half an hour. Matthews then signaled to me to approach. I stepped out of my hiding place and walked into their camp. The two men who had attacked me spoke animatedly to the others, possibly describing the afternoon of our encounter. They gestured wildly with their arms and smiled.

The first thing I noticed upon entering their camp was the overwhelming stench emanating from it and the waste, both human and animal, scattered around the humpy. This and what appeared to be a plague of flies was almost more than I could bear. It was twice as bad as the stench of the *Havring*. I later learned that the smell was fish oil. Due to their lack of hygiene, the flies were attracted to them by the thousands. By smearing the fish oil onto their heads, they kept the flies at bay. Standing before them I asked Matthews whether he could handle the smell.

"Let me put it to you this way," he said. "I think it's a lot better than having to dodge flying spears."

I laughed at his joke and, mimicking us, so did the aboriginals.

The aboriginals are an amazingly resilient people. They live off the land in the truest sense of the meaning. They grind plants called *nardoo* down into a fine paste and use it to bake cakes. They eat lizards and practically any animal that moves in the bush. They survive the heat and cold dressed minimally. They are truly a remarkable but primitive race.

We stayed with them for two hours. We communicated by hand movement and occasional scratchings made in the sand with twigs. Matthews drew a crude picture of a man with a spear throwing it at another. He then made a cross over it to signify his opposition to such action. Next to this scratching he drew another picture depicting an aboriginal and a white man sitting peacefully together. The reaction to this was positive. They had not only understood the message but agreed with it as well.

They accompanied us to our horses, chattering among themselves as we rode off. Matthews was extremely pleased with the encounter and hoped that it would serve him well in the future.

As time passed we became quite friendly with the aboriginals. It didn't take long before we were communicating in English. Their ability to mimic and learn quickly quite amazed me. The two young men who had attacked me became so friendly that at times they'd lead stray sheep back into the property. As long as we didn't encroach on their sacred land, all was well.

I have always been surprised by the attitude of white men when it comes to settlement. They grab huge tracts of land, slice it up with avarice, and then go and shoot dead a black man who has the temerity to suggest it belonged to him. As far as the new settlers are concerned, inhabiting a land for thousands of years counts for nothing. The black men are ignorant, dirty primitives who should be grateful they are given warning before being shot.

Wherever the white men have explored, they have left behind them a trail of destruction. Contact between white men and the aboriginal has proved fatal even in those rare instances when they have been treated fairly, for white men not only brought new foods and customs with them, but diseases as well. The aboriginals were little prepared to deal with such things and are still paying the price today. If disease and subsequent death hasn't dwindled their number, then turning to drink—an imported scourge—has turned them into social incorrigibles.

The tribe living on the outskirts of Matthews' property numbered approximately sixty when we first came to know them. Recently I met one of their warriors. There are less than a dozen from his tribe left today, he told me. Most died of disease. Others met their deaths more violently after being chased like dogs by a party of white men who were looking for something different to hunt. He was going to retreat back into the outback of the country and spend the remainder of his days in solitude.

"You white people treat the land bad, Mr. Moses," he told me. "Some of you want to do good, but when a white man does good it's bad for us blackfellas."

Poor "blackfellas"! I pray for them and hope that Hashem created the great Australian land mass large enough for them to escape from the white man's greedy nature.

Chapter 9

My wife and children arrived in Australia exactly ten days before the Pesach of 1850. I can remember being nervous and unusually restless that day. Passengers were due to disembark late morning and I was eager to leave for the docks as soon as the sun arose. I davened and then saw to the horses, not bothering with breakfast. I fed and groomed them, prepared the carriage, and was soon ready to leave. I impatiently waited for Matthews who, accustomed to dealing with such matters, was to accompany me to the docks. He, at least, was in no rush to go anywhere. We finally left the property and arrived at the docks half an hour before the ship's arrival.

The last time I'd been on the docks I was a different man, a man bereft of dignity. True, I still hadn't been granted emancipation, but my situation was far from bad. Matthews had helped me enormously by treating me humanely. I became particularly aware of my good fortune when I caught sight of some of the newly convicted men on deck that morning.

By eleven we could see the ship come into sight. I almost shook from excitement as she loomed larger into view.

My eyes scanned the deck for a glimpse of my loved ones and I soon caught sight of them. I yelled in their direction. Their heads turned and they waved back enthusiastically. Twenty minutes later they were by my side. Tears streamed down my wife's face and mine. In the flurry of events, I happened to catch sight of Matthews who, I noticed, had also shed a tear on our behalf.

Rachel looked beaten and drawn from the passage, but was full of spirit and thrilled to be reunited with me after such a difficult year and a half. The twins, Rivkah and Yaakov, were rather dazed and overwhelmed by the course of events. At first they were unsure of who I was or where they were. I couldn't blame them, for they were only approaching the age of six.

Matthews took to the children immediately, and they to him, and after we'd left the docks he had them up front, flanking him in the carriage.

My wife has always been a flexible woman who tries her best to adapt to any circumstance. And yet it didn't take much to guess that she would have been happier settled in a town close to a Jewish community. As we headed back to the property, I promised her that should the opportunity eventually arise, when I could start out on my own, we'd move to Melbourne where she would find a semblance of Jewish life as she knew it.

Masters and Coulhoun quickly left their work stations when they heard the carriage pull in through the property gates. Time would show them courteous to Rachel and kind to the children. When Darcy brought the sheep in later that day, he made his way to our little shack and made his introductions.

"Don't mind me saying, Mrs. Lazar, but you've a fine husband. We've had our rows since he came to us, but he's changed my attitude in more ways than one."

"Thank you, Mr. Darcy." And then, turning to me, she said, "Moses, do we have something for Mr. Darcy to drink? He looks very thirsty." This brought a smile to his dusty face.

"The first day your husband arrived and we came to introduce ourselves, he offered us the same hospitality you just did," he laughed. "Who learned from whom?"

"Neither I from my wife nor my wife from me," I answered. "We have to thank the Almighty for having taught us how to welcome guests," I replied.

Even with all our happiness at being a family once again, our situation was difficult. The most pressing question was what to do with the children. My wife and I had to devise a learning schedule for them. They would easily occupy themselves on the property, but they needed some form of supervised education as well.

The day after we returned to the property, Matthews came to our rooms for discussion. He came straight to the point. He had promised me much, my freedom included, and he was proud that he was a man of his word. He had documented my progress and wished to hand papers and his personal recommendation to the governor's offices. He didn't expect any problems and hoped I'd give him a month's notice if I intended to depart.

I knew Matthews didn't want me to leave. Yet he was an extremely honest man who would stand by his promise. It was too early to ask my wife's opinion. She was a stranger to Australia, and her major worry was keeping the children safely out of the creek that ran through the back of the property.

I knew how much Matthews depended on me and I felt that I owed him a favor in return. The only question I had was how long my wife could last living in the bush. For all I knew, in the long run she might have enjoyed it. As for me, I enjoyed the quiet country life but felt so much more complete when I knew there was a synagogue and other Jews within walking distance.

These were the things which ran through my mind after Matthews left our room. Neither Matthews nor I need have worried ourselves about the question though, for events totally beyond our control would soon change the lives of all of us on the property.

I decided to defer the question of our future until after Pesach. There were only a few days left before the holiday and my wife took to cleaning all our belongings and our small quarters as though she was at war with them.

After four days in Australia, she looked a different woman. The color had returned to her cheeks and the drawn look across her brow had disappeared. She told me that she finally felt liberated from London. Now she realized how the overcrowding and filth of Stepney and Whitechapel had depressed her for years. The great vastness of the countryside outside Melbourne was proving to be the best medicine for her.

As for the children, we'd never seen them happier. They played games all day long, chasing wild chickens from one corner of the yard to the other and then back again. They would come to watch me work, meddle with the cook's implements in the kitchen, and then hold on tightly to the reins as Matthews took them for rides around the yard on his horse. In the evenings, after I'd finished with my work, I would sit them down in front of me and teach them stories from the Torah and *mishnayos*.

Our first Shabbos in Australia was the most peaceful we'd ever spent together. The chicken which I had slaughtered before Shabbos was the most delicious I had ever eaten. Rachel made a soup out of the feet and neck and baked the remainder with whatever vegetables the cook gave her. During the meal we could see the light coming from Matthews' rooms.

"He's a lonely man, isn't he?" said Rachel.

"But a good one at that," I replied.

"His treatment of you is quite miraculous. Why do you think he does it?" she asked.

"I've thought about it often enough," I said. "Sometimes I feel as if I'm living parts of his life for him."

Matthews was now looking through his window across the pastures towards Melbourne. He looked melancholy. I told Rachel of the strange meeting between Matthews and the white-bearded gentleman.

"I know him well, but he guards himself furiously when I come too close. He's hiding behind a secret that is haunting him. Whenever I ask just one question too many he begins ordering me around like one of the other employees."

We had been invited to spend Pesach with the Hart family and the newly appointed rabbi, Rabbi Rintel, in Melbourne.

Matthews allowed us use of his carriage to travel. Before leaving the property, we looked for Matthews to bid him farewell. I must have searched for over an hour without success. It was most unlike him, particularly since he had become so attached to the children. We couldn't wait any longer and soon were on our way to Melbourne.

We drove directly to Rabbi Rintel's residence, where his wife informed me that her husband was at the Harts' place baking matzahs in the new oven bought specifically for that purpose. It was a short walk and my wife suggested I take the children with me. Off we marched, and a jollier trio was not to be found on all the streets of Melbourne that day.

At the Harts' home we found Rabbi Rintel busy baking matzahs with two helpers. I soon joined their ranks while the younger members of the Hart family, who'd come to watch the process, entertained Yaakov and Rivkah.

At the far end of the table sat one man, who poured a mixture of water and flour into a steel bowl. He furiously thrashed his hands about the bowl, mixing the two ingredients together. After a minute he was left with a solid mass. He then stood opposite the other helper. They each took an end of a very long rolling pin. Together, in what I could only describe as a rowing movement, they kneaded the mixture until it took the form of a smooth paste. This stage in the process took maybe three minutes. They were in a rush, for the matzahs had to be completed in a matter of minutes.

They then sliced pieces off the dough and rolled them into circles with smaller rolling pins. Before passing them on to Rabbi Rintel, who was eagerly awaiting them at the open oven, they poked holes into each one. Rabbi Rintel then took a long pole which had a tray attached at one end. He scooped up the thin slices and placed them in the oven. He had to be quick because it took less than thirty seconds before the matzahs were baked. After they had finished baking, the rabbi took them out of the oven and placed them onto another table. The entire procedure couldn't have taken longer than six or seven minutes.

We spent the remainder of the day baking matzahs. Rabbi Rintel was baking enough for the entire Jewish population in the colony. Throughout the day members of the community came to the Hart house to pick them up. In addition, Rabbi Rintel sought volunteers to distribute matzahs to householders who, in Rabbi Rintel's words, "may not keep the festival as God would want it." He was not pointing an accusing finger at them, he was simply concerned for their spiritual welfare. His hopes were that they would accept the matzahs and possibly even come to refrain from eating any forms of *chametz* during the festival. His heart was with every member of the community.

I had spent the previous Pesach aboard the *Havring*. Then, I hadn't been too certain of the exact dates of Pesach. I therefore refrained from eating bread for two weeks to satisfy myself. Those two weeks were possibly the worst of the entire voyage. Seder night is a time for Jews to break off into small family groups and withdraw into our houses to celebrate our exodus from Egypt. And yet there I was, tossed on the uncaring sea, sailing farther and farther away from my loved ones.

There couldn't have been a greater contrast between the Pesach of 1849 and 1850. The former was the most miserable I'd ever spent, while the latter was the most spiritually uplifting I can remember. The entire Hart family came to the seder at the rabbi's house. Both my children sang the *Mah Nishtanah*. They stood on their chairs, and although they began shyly, they soon found confidence. Rachel cried out of sheer happiness. As for me, I did my best not to look at her, for if I had kept my eyes on her too long, I, too, would have broken into tears.

We sat up late. The rabbi told many stories of

Pesach. My wife spoke of the years of poverty in London when obtaining all the required ingredients for the seder table was often impossible.

By the time we'd finished singing the last tunes from the Haggadah it was nearly two o'clock. A few hours later I was in shul.

I recall standing at the back of the synagogue thanking Hashem. I had had faith in Him, and my family had been restored to me. My dreams had borne fruit. Could a happier man be found in the colony? I asked myself.

My happiness, however, proved to be short-lived.

Chapter 10

There was a fierce wind blowing the day after Pesach when we returned to the property, and as we made our way along the rough road, the blackest, most ominous-looking clouds seemed to chase us along the way. As we rode into the stables, I could sense all was not well. There were Darcy, Masters, and Coulhoun clustered together, talking in the middle of a work day. Instead of ranging through the pastureland, the sheep were penned in tightly against each other, bleating. Even Coulhoun's simple face looked bleak.

Matthews appeared out of nowhere and as he walked by I needed no telling that he was in a black mood. Maybe he had seen us, maybe he hadn't; in any case, he paid no attention to us.

"What's the matter, Darcy?" I asked.

"The sheep are dropping like flies. The day after you left we lost five. The numbers have been increasing ever since," he said softly.

I knew there was nothing to be done in such a situation. All one could hope for was that the plague which was killing the sheep stopped before it destroyed the entire flock.

It wasn't to be. By the end of the day thirty more sheep had died. The number of deaths remained constant for three days. Then, as if by pact, in two days over three hundred sheep died. The sight was unbelievable. Carcasses lay strewn across the pen, heads thrown back grotesquely, legs thrust forward. The stench was unbearable and with it came great armies of flies milling around in thousands. Matthews hovered around us throughout the week never speaking as we dug trenches for the sheep and buried them in shallow graves. Where once there were hundreds of sheep now remained none.

We all knew only too well what it meant for us. We would have to find work elsewhere. For Masters and Darcy, still government men, the future looked even bleaker. They talked about staying on in the bush, having become accustomed to its serenity, but this would be difficult as Darcy and Masters both wished to marry.

This wasn't as easy as it sounded. The number of males in the colony far outnumbered the females. Convicted men like Darcy and Masters would have a hard time of it. Indeed, from what I'd been told, most of the convicted men in the colony did not marry. Years later I was to catch up with Masters, who, much to my surprise, had found a young woman to settle down with. Darcy and Coulhoun, so Masters told me, hadn't been as lucky.

As far as my family and I were concerned, there was no choice but to return to Melbourne. We had a little money but weren't foolish enough to think it would take us far.

One morning, as we were trying to decide on our future course, Matthews got on his horse and rode out without a word to any of us. We watched him gallop past, his eyes fixed firmly on the ground somewhere ahead of him. He didn't point the reins in the direction of Melbourne. Instead, he turned his great brown mare in the opposite direction, into the bush. As I watched him ride through the gates, I had a premonition that he wouldn't return, but I decided to wait for him nonetheless.

I walked into Matthews' rooms searching for a clue to his intentions. I combed every square inch and the only thing of interest I found was a small diary he had kept. It was written in a meticulous hand, entries neatly dated at the top of each page. I read it through and was surprised that he never once alluded to his moods. Rather, he'd enter fact upon fact about what was or wasn't accomplished on the property, as well as jotting down his daily transactions. I detected a feeling of detachment in his writing. Somehow I got the impression that it had been nothing but a game for him. It seemed that his heart hadn't been in it.

Everything about the diary was orderly except that

one page was missing. The date meant nothing to me until I read the entry before. It then dawned on me that the entry referred to the day he had met the white-bearded gentleman in the city. I could see from the paper's jagged edge that it had been torn out of the notebook, not neatly as one would think, but with great force. Intriguing as this was, it didn't help in solving the problem at hand.

After four days with no sight of Matthews, Darcy, Masters, Coulhoun, and the cook decided they'd best serve themselves looking for employment elsewhere. We had a small farewell party for them. My wife cooked them a most delicious meal, but when we came to eat it, none of us seemed to have an appetite.

We had had our ups and downs, particularly Darcy, Masters, and myself. Ours had been a shaky but mutually respectful relationship, particularly after their change of attitude months earlier when I was suspicious they were in cahoots with Jack O'Hearn.

As they made to leave, my family and I walked them to the property gates. They fidgeted with their belongings, finding it difficult to say goodbye to us.

"Will you come back and visit us soon, Mr. James?" Rivkah asked Masters.

"Do come soon," added Yaakov. "We'll be waiting for you when you do. And Mr. Darcy will take us for a ride on his back."

The men were not accustomed to showing their emotions and excused themselves, saying they wished to be in Melbourne before nightfall. As they bid us farewell, I said to them, "You won't be running into Jack O'Hearn by any chance?"

"When we do we'll tell him you've crossed Australia westward," answered Masters.

"And may your good Lord bear witness, Moses Lazar, that as long as I'm alive I'll never speak anything but kind words about you and your good family," said Darcy.

"Never a truer word spoken," agreed Masters.

"Me, too!" said Coulhoun, impressing the seriousness of this short phrase by standing to attention.

As they walked away, I was overcome by a feeling of sadness. A bond that had attached us to the land and to each other had been broken. I watched them walk away, and when they had disappeared from sight I rejoined my family, walked inside the gates, and shut them behind us.

The questions at hand were manifold. How long were we to wait? Where exactly were we to direct the limited manpower we had? How long could we keep the children occupied while both Rachel and I worked? An even greater question begged. It is true that the members of the Jewish community were few in number, but how long should we, a religious family, stay away from the center of Jewish communal life in the colony, seeing we had the choice to do as we pleased? Was it better for us to have everything we wanted materially, only to suffer spiritually? Or was it better for us to live with less and yet have access to an existing, albeit spiritually frail, community? There was no alternative. We had to leave. Both Rachel and I realized this. Our only concern was that, having been so decently treated by Matthews, did we not owe him a favor in return?

We came to a compromise. We would stay for a month, two at the most. Should Matthews fail to materialize from the bush within that time, we would take his livestock and all his belongings to Melbourne and ask the rabbi what should be done with them.

Not a week after the men had left us, the weather turned bitterly cold. The rains, heavier than any I'd seen since arriving in the colony, were torrential and ceased only intermittently over a two week period. The property became one large pool of disgusting mud. The children were kept indoors and grew bored and restless. The three cows strayed and a dozen of the twenty chickens died from the cold.

I located the cows on a day when thunder and lightning caused two of the three horses to bolt in fright. I was too tired to chase them and the following day, when I did venture out after them, I had no luck at all. I attempted to find the aboriginals to help me, but they had, as was customary for them, shifted camp. That night, nearly three weeks after Matthews had left us, we decided to move into town. We planned to move as soon as the weather cleared.

And so it was that on a Sunday, a blustery, grey day in July 1850, I led my family away from George Matthews' property towards Melbourne. Following our carriage was one horse and three thinning cows. We were going to start life again in Melbourne.

Chapter 11

We made our way to Hart's place in Melbourne. We arrived at nightfall and were greeted by Hart at the door. He was as gracious as ever but, with a house full of guests, he hadn't room for us. He could see that the children were tired and he quickly called for one of his servants to run ahead and inform Rabbi Rintel that we'd be staying the night. Rabbi Rintel and his wife made us as comfortable as they could in their cramped study.

The hard grind of life began the following morning. Hart came to visit us and I informed both he and the rabbi that we didn't expect to be showered with charity. My priorities were clear. I wished to find lodgings for my family and get a job. On the subject of what to do with Matthews' few possessions, the rabbi suggested we sell them and put the money in an account for Matthews, should he ever show up and need it. Hart said he would glady purchase the merchandise.

That day I succeeded in finding lodgings some two miles from the synagogue. They were run down, but still a far sight better than anything my wife and I had lived in in England. After two days of cleaning and scrubbing, the rooms looked quite livable.

We arranged for Yaakov to learn with Rabbi Rintel every morning. Rivkah stayed home with Rachel, who taught her how to read and write Hebrew. As for me, I had been given a recommendation by Asher Hart to a few gentlemen of business. I spent my days wandering from one to another looking for work. Yet wherever I went I was out of luck. This went on for some time. Employment wasn't available. The main reason was that a few boats had recently docked, and the men coming off them had found the jobs I was now seeking.

The weeks passed, and with all avenues exhausted, I decided to start a small business of my own. My wife and I both knew how to sew. I thought I'd utilize this skill and begin tailoring.

We purchased some fabric, thread, and needles. Together we worked day and night, and after a month we had tailored twenty pairs of pants. I tried to strike a deal with some of the local Jewish merchants. They were willing to take our work but weren't too hopeful about our prospects for success. We waited for a few weeks, but the results were not promising. Only three pairs of trousers had been sold.

Around this time I met a young merchant from Sydney who told me he had some rabbit furs for sale at a very good price. I had thousands of possible projects running through my head, and the thought of owning a sack of rabbit furs didn't strike me as strange. I didn't know what I'd do with them, but I purchased them nonetheless.

I bought back one of Matthews' horses from Hart and began a small delivery service. As this brought in just a pittance, I only delivered goods during the morning hours. In the afternoon I either looked for work or offered my services to anyone who needed odd jobs done.

During this time in my life, I was so full of ambition, endeavor, and enterprise that I never found the time to look at myself objectively. What I didn't realize was that I was so bound up in attempting to succeed that the Torah life I had managed to cling to through the most adverse circumstances began to suffer.

It is brought down in *seforim* that only two know the level of a man's *kedushah*: Hashem and the man's wife. If a woman feels that her husband is not on an acceptable level of *kedushah*, she must admonish him and make him aware of his failings. When Korach began his conflict with Moshe, the wife of On ben Peles, an *eishes chayil*, warned her husband that his meddling would bring him no good. She saved him from the same fate that awaited Korach and his minions. By the same token, Korach's wife could have saved her husband, but she only forced him deeper into conflict with Moshe Rabbeinu.

Hashem, in His infinite kindness, gave me the most

wonderful wife. My Rachel, may she live to one hundred and twenty, like On ben Peles's wife, came to my rescue during a spiritual crisis. At first she watched me cautiously as I desperately made an effort to find some success in life. She wanted me to succeed more than anyone. But the result of my frantic pace brought unwelcome repercussions to our household. I paid little attention to the education of the children, satisfied that the rabbi and Rachel were doing a good job with both of them. I brought no Torah home even when I had the strength to do so. All I had on my mind were the horse's shoes, rabbit furs, faulty trousers, and how to cross the muddy streets of Melbourne as fast as I could.

It was on a Friday afternoon in the middle of a windy July winter that Rachel put my priorities in order. She described what I had become in less than encouraging words. She told me that it was enough that she had had to suffer without me for the year and a half of our separation. She would not now face a life of spiritual barrenness with me. There were tears in her eyes as she spoke. All she wanted was to do what was best for us, to retain the framework that would guide us through life.

"I'd rather be poor as we were in England," she said, "than see our Yiddishkeit fall by the wayside. There I never had the need to speak out like this, Moses. Life in England might have been difficult, but at least you were close to the other members of our community. Just being part of a God-fearing congregation was enough to have you bring home the love and wisdom of God. Australia is a different land. You have been remarkable in staying close to the ways of Hashem, but there are parts of you that need to be brought to the surface again."

She opened up the doors of *teshuvah* for me, and with Elul approaching, I had the perfect opportunity to make amends.

I spent that Shabbos deep in thought. There was no denying any of Rachel's observations. The question was what I was going to do about them. I decided to cease some of my endeavors and instead sit and learn Torah for several hours each day.

When I had given the responsibility for *parnasah* back to whom it belonged—Hashem—He took good care of me. From out of nowhere a ridiculous but intriguing idea came to me. Why not, I thought to myself, go back into tailoring? I would make cheap rain jackets and attach the rabbit furs the merchant had sold me to the collars and sleeves.

It was late August and we had little time left before the winter season ended. Rachel and I worked furiously, and within a few days we had fifteen rain jackets ready to sell. I raced back down to the merchants, who were impressed with the quality and design. Two days later one of the merchants came knocking on our door at ten o'clock at night. He'd sold the five jackets we'd given him and wanted more. The following day two other merchants made similar requests.

Over the next week Rachel and I worked harder

than we'd ever worked in our lives. Together we sat in our small sitting room tailoring fur-trimmed rain jackets. Before we started work I would learn three *mishnayos* and a chapter of Chumash. I would then tell it over to Rachel as we cut and stitched throughout the day.

Melbourne's weather is unreliable. In mid-summer, one day can be hot enough to broil your skin and the next day it can rain in torrents. Thus, rain jackets are never out of season. Overnight we'd become quite well-to-do. We weren't rich, but at last we were in a position where we didn't have to worry about our money running out.

Rosh Hashanah of 1850 saw a better meal on our table than we'd ever eaten in our lives. I purchased a duck and a goose and *shechted* them, and Rachel *kashered* and cooked them. I bought my wife two new dresses and bonnets to match, and fitted out our little twins in new clothes.

We may have looked like a royal family and we may have eaten like one, but that Rosh Hashanah still remains embedded in my mind as one of our most special mainly because we were able to fulfill a great mitzvah. We ushered three guests recently arrived from England into our house. Both Rachel and I felt elated at being able to provide them with the same type of hospitality that we'd been showered with since arriving in Melbourne.

I don't wish to describe the *chagim* of 1850 at length. Suffice to say that my place in the congregation had become cemented and that I had been appointed assistant to Rabbi Rintel in matters relating to the running of the synagogue. The holidays passed quietly except for two noteworthy incidents.

The first was a discussion I had with my wife during the Ten Days of Repentance. Our comfortable position in life aside, she longed to see her family again. Months earlier she'd written to them begging them to show interest in coming to Australia. Her family then consisted of her mother, her father, and two unmarried sisters. When their reply came, it sent Rachel into deep depression. They wanted to be with us but couldn't contemplate the arduous passage over. The letter couldn't have come at a worse time. Only days earlier Rachel told me that she was with child, and physically she felt tired and unwell.

The second incident occurred on Simchas Torah. I was aware that a stranger had been davening with us since the first day of Sukkos. He would appear soon after the beginning of every minyan and leave moments before it ended. This was most peculiar. He was an older man, and although I couldn't place his face, something about him was familiar. Hart drew my attention to the fact that the fellow wouldn't talk to anyone other than to say that he'd come from Sydney on business and was here to pray and not pass his time in idle chatter.

I was curious, I'll admit, and on Simchas Torah I decided to speak to him. I noticed that he wasn't at all pleased in my addressing him. What's more, I recognized the fire in his eyes. It was the same gentleman who'd spat at Matthews nearly a year earlier.

"I seem to remember you, sir," I said, introducing myself. "I used to work for George Matthews." The man's eyes lit up, more out of spite than curiosity. He said nothing. "He disappeared into the bush some months ago and hasn't been heard from since," I continued.

"Let the hound remain there," he abruptly answered.

"Why do you call him a hound?" I asked. But I'd pushed my luck too far. The fellow told me to mind my own business and leave him be.

Who was I to argue with him? I did as he bid me, still curious as to what deep secret surrounded both Matthews and the man with the long beard standing in front of me.

Chapter 12

The harder we worked, the more successful we were, and this invigorated us. It was as though we'd been given a new lease on life. As Rachel's pregnancy progressed, I couldn't help but think how lucky I was that Hashem had sent me to Australia in the first place. We were happy and healthy, free to reside in a country where it was possible to start with nothing in life and actually get somewhere. It had taken enormous strength and faith, but we had somehow succeeded. And, most important, we had not been forced to leave our beliefs and traditions behind.

I soon became quite a proficient tailor and worked long hours to keep up with the orders that increasingly came our way. With Rachel's help we produced garments that couldn't be matched in the colony for their quality or style. At the same time, I was more than content to work at home and be in constant contact with my family.

With my mind free of worry about how we were to survive, I was able to devote more attention to learning. I found a willing partner in Rabbi Rintel. There were many occasions when we'd sit up to all hours of the morning, our heads bent over a Talmud or Chumash. I would learn at his house, walking there after a long day, and return home anywhere between midnight and three in the morning.

I had to pass through the central streets of Melbourne on my way to the rabbi's house. This was always an experience.

In those days Melbourne wasn't a big town. Most of the prosperity and excitement of Australian life was to be found in the country's biggest settlement, Botany Bay. For the rougher elements of Melbourne's population, there was only one means of solace, excitement, and entertainment: alcohol.

Watching grown men drink until they become inebriated beyond consciousness has always amazed and frightened me. I have never understood what causes men to drink more than is good for them. I have heard it said that men do it out of oppression, boredom, anger, or unhappiness. The list goes on. And yet, do men not see what drink does to them? A drunken man becomes irrational and many a time involved in drunken brawls. Go past any drinking establishment on an evening and you will not have long to wait before a melee begins. These noisy bouts are horrendous affairs and men are severely beaten, waking up out of their stupor hours later not remembering how or why they came to have such bruised and heavy heads. The irony of it all is that they return the following night to go through the same ritual again.

It was in this atmosphere that we lived. We did our best to feign ignorance of the seedier side of life—going through our city as if we were wearing blinders. Even today, years after Melbourne has settled down as a most respectable town, there are occasions when I am frightened to allow my children outdoors. I suppose this is the price one has to pay when living in a frontier land.

Since coming to Australia, I have sometimes had a helpless feeling of isolation, like a man stranded on an island. I often ponder the hypothetical question of whether I would have come out to the colony if given the free choice to do so. Life here can be materially beneficial, and yet one must live within a weak Jewish community. If, however, one chooses to stay in England, the community is strong, but the opportunities are limited and the air of London stifling.

What person could reject the offer of a new land, a healthy living, and good conditions for his family? Yet there is so much at stake when the very essence of your life, your Yiddishkeit, is laid on the line.

If someone were given such a choice tomorrow, what would he do? Tell him the future of his children is doubtful and he may reply that such problems should be faced when the time arises. Or he might realize the truths being spoken and take heed by not venturing to such a faraway place.

Do you need to walk the streets at night knowing that some drunken, foul-mouthed larrikin might beat you to a hair's breadth of your life? Need you worry that your children will suffer because they haven't other Jewish children to play and learn with?

The truth is that anyone with common sense would hesitate before making such a decision. Ah, and I can see the reader of this journal, my dear descendant, remarking to himself that I have mentioned time and time again that I was happy in this foreign land. The reader would be correct in making such an observation. But the reader must remember that I, his ancestor, was sent here as a common thief, and that a complete pardon allowing me to return to my native England was granted only many years after I'd settled, after I had watched two of my children marry. By then it was too late to uproot my entire family, my wife's family, pack our bags, and return to England. My family had seen enough turmoil over the years to see any more.

Besides, Rachel would never hear of us returning. The very thought of London made her ill.

I can be a very heavy sleeper when the occasion suits me. If I've worked solidly all day, I will fall asleep almost immediately and, as my dear wife tells me, need a bucket of ice cold water to be woken from my slumber.

At three o'clock on a Wednesday morning in the second week of March, 1851, I was rudely awakened by Rachel. She had tried waking me in every conceivable manner, all to no avail. She finally threw some water from her drinking cup into my face. You can imagine my reaction. For a moment I thought I was back on the *Havring*, being doused in seawater. I shouted out in fright but calmed down at the sound of my wife's voice.

"Moses, run to Rabbi Rintel's house and get his wife."

I jumped out of bed, wide awake. Mrs. Rintel was our midwife, and if my wife was calling for her in the middle of the night, it could mean only one thing: she was about to give birth!

In my haste I pulled a shirt and trousers on over my pajamas. As I was tying up my boots, I asked Rachel, "I realize it's an emergency, my dear, but don't I deserve being woken up in a decent manner?"

"You do," she replied. "But were I to continue trying to do so, you'd be woken by the screams of a newborn baby."

I harnessed the horse to the carriage and rode to the rabbi's house as fast as the beast's legs would carry me. The rabbi opened the door for me and quickly instructed his wife to dress immediately.

At seven twenty-five, five hours after I'd run out to fetch Mrs. Rintel, Rachel gave birth to our third child, a girl, whom we named Sarah. I was called into the room soon after the birth and sat by the bed looking at my wife's radiant face as she warmly cuddled our beautiful child. Then, quite out of character, I began to cry. Once I started, I couldn't stop. These were tears of happiness. I was so thankful to Hashem for our healthy, round-faced little child and that Rachel hadn't had to suffer through too difficult a labor. I must have looked a sight, a hefty man towering over six feet in height, a physical giant among men, crying his eyes out like a baby.

Let me make it clear that I am proud to tell the story and never fail to mention it before other men. And why not? There is nothing to be ashamed of in shedding a tear. Of course, I try not to make a habit of it.

Yaakov and Rivkah were thrilled to have a little sister and went out of their way to help with the chores around the house. What a blessing they were. There were times when they could have spent their hours enjoying themselves but chose instead to help their mother carry the burden of the household. This was comforting to Rachel because she didn't have her mother to help her. Her mother's absence preyed on her mind, and she became all the more determined to convince her family to come out to Australia. Once again she wrote a long, passionate letter to England begging them to make the passage.

By the year 1851 the speed of mail had increased unbelievably. If the connections were right, a return letter from England might find its way to you after only six or seven months. It was late in October when the expected reply came. I picked it up at the postal office and practically ran all the way home. I couldn't bear to see Rachel so miserable and prayed that her family would agree to come out.

I simply placed the letter on the small reading desk in front of her. When she realized what it was, she went to snap it up, but hesitated for a moment, fearing that the answer to her plea would be negative. Slowly she slit open the envelope and took out the letter.

I watched her pore over the page and breathed a great sigh of relief as her eyes lit up in happiness. Her family had decided to come after all.

Their plan was to arrive in Melbourne late September, 1852, about a year away. My wife wished they could have arrived earlier, but when we considered that it took three months to send money to them to purchase their tickets and three months for traveling, eleven months wasn't so long a wait. No amount of time was too long if it meant that Rachel would be happy.

Until they arrived we continued on in our enterprising way. There was nothing we could complain about and everything to thank Hashem for. Yes, our lives proceeded along happily until a month before Rachel's family arrived.

Early in the September of 1852, I was inside cutting some fabric when I heard the twins raise the alarm. I raced outside to smell the choking fumes of smoke. I could hear the crackling sound of fire coming from the side of the house. It was there that I met the twins. They were trying to put out the fire, which started, so they later told me, when our neighbor had burned some rubbish in his yard. A breeze had fanned the fire onto the fence running along the middle of the two properties, and it had caught the side of the house.

There was no point in battling the blaze because the fire had spread so rapidly. By this time Rachel had come outside with Sarah. Assured that my family was safe, I raced inside and grabbed my *tefillin*. With the smoke growing thicker, I then grabbed a large amount of money that we had kept hidden in the hallway. Finally, I raced out, not a moment too soon.

Our neighbor, a hearty chap but a trifle light-headed, came out to offer his sincerest apologies. It was obliging of him but not quite appreciated, seeing everything we owned had just turned into cinder.

Chapter 13

Eighteen hundred and fifty-one will be forever remembered by me and thousands of others as a major turning point in Australian history. It was the year when Australia began to throw off the yoke of a colonial backwater and took the first steps towards recognition throughout the world as a country for more than just luckless convicts.

Having worn out his luck on the Californian goldfields, a man by the name of Hargraves returned to his native Australia with the intention of finding gold. To everyone's surprise, he did! His lucky strike was in the northern state of New South Wales. The news of the great find was announced in the May of that year.

Gold fever swept through the colony. The repercussions were enormous. In Melbourne we read with great interest and watched as many would be "men of wealth" made their way northwards. It was a kind of mass hypnosis. The mere thought of wealth was enough to make men lose all sense of themselves.

Melbourne hadn't yet been affected, but as the months passed and it became apparent that the prospectors weren't going to leave a stone unturned until every last speck of gold dust had been mined from the earth, men from all over Australia packed up their belongings for the goldfields. The exodus had devastating effects upon the local economy. Many businesses closed overnight.

In September of 1852, a man named John Dunlop discovered a massive field of gold only seventy-five miles outside Melbourne, in a place called Ballarat. But before we come to Ballarat and its development, which so changed my own life, let me relate how at the time of Dunlop's famous discovery I could be found only miles away from the man himself.

The fire which burned down our premises was devastating. Overnight we became homeless wanderers. That night we had to seek shelter once again with some hospitable congregant. Thankfully, our position as members of the community was such that people were only too willing to help. Families whom we'd bestowed hospitality upon willingly returned the favor.

As far as Rachel was concerned, this couldn't have occurred at a worse time. She had planned for her family's arrival to the last detail and she was thrown quite out of kilter. To make recompense for our losses, I soon found furnished lodgings which were bigger in size than those we'd previously rented.

I then had to make arrangements for getting back

into business as quickly as I could. I had enjoyed the freedom of being my own master and planned to continue where I'd left off before the fire. The money I had retrieved from the house was sufficient for my needs. Three days after the fire I was ready to buy material. But then, as had so often happened in my life, things took an unexpected turn.

Unlike the first time I had sought work in Melbourne, when word of the disaster spread I was immediately offered two positions. One was as a salesman in a merchant store. The proprietor, Solomon Benjamin, had known me since my arrival in Melbourne and we had struck up a friendly accord. The other offer was much more mysterious. It came in the form of a letter which arrived from England exactly one day before our home was burned to the ground.

I had gone to the postal office to collect my mail. The postal clerk handed me a letter addressed to the Melbourne Hebrew Congregation. I took the envelope and delivered it to Rabbi Rintel.

I sat opposite him at his desk as he opened it. He sat there for what seemed an age, reading and rereading the missive. After a while he lifted his eyes and, without a word, handed me the letter. It read:

> Urgent: May the person who locates the whereabouts of one Yankel Meisels, aged 36, last heard of residing approximately 60 miles west of Melbourne, claim the money herein and reply at first mail to A.E.M. London Central.

Together we discussed the mystery. We had never heard the name before and further investigation failed to uncover the identity of "one Yankel Meisels." Our discussion led us along the following line of reasoning. Firstly, seeing the letter had been addressed to the Melbourne Hebrew Congregation, we assumed that the writer was Jewish. The word "urgent," thickly scrawled at the top of the page, indicated that whoever he was, Yankel Meisels was sorely missed by the sender. Any Jew with a good heart could not allow such a request to go unheeded. It was therefore incumbent upon us to make some form of inquiry as to this Meisels' whereabouts.

Rabbi Rintel took the matter to the synagogue board which met later that week, three days after the fire. He suggested that we send a party out to look for the fellow. At first the suggestion was regarded as foolhardy. Australia was so large, came the objection, that it would be like trying to find a grain of sand on a beach. Asher Hart, however, thought differently. He proposed that I be sent out on behalf of the congregation for a period of two weeks in search of the man. It was an act of *chessed*, he explained. He reasoned that I was familiar with the area, knew how to survive out in the bush, and could handle myself better than most men out there. I would be funded through the synagogue. His influence hadn't lessened over the years, and soon he had the entire board of six members agreeing to his proposal.

The offer put me in a difficult situation. When the board suggested it, I was left dumbstruck. I finally explained to them that my position was terribly unsettled. I had lost everything I owned and had to prepare for the arrival of family from England. The board members all jumped at me, offering to help out in whatever way they could. The children would be seen to, my wife would be comforted. They were, in short, at my disposal.

The offer was hard to refuse. I spoke to my wife who, after a short period of deliberation, meekly gave her consent. The decision was easier for her to make because of the luck we'd had in finding accommodations: a three room house only a ten minute walk from the center of town.

My first reaction to the news of my appointment was joy that I could perform an important mitzvah. Whoever this Yankel Meisels was, there were people who were concerned about him. What's more, as Asher Hart had pointed out, I knew the terrain well enough, and if there was someone to be found, I would have a good chance of finding him.

The synagogue board acted as though they were sending out a fully equipped expedition to the middle of unknown parts. For many of these city bred men, my two week odyssey into the bush would rival the journeys of the great Venetian traveler Marco Polo. Their talk amused me, for there was nothing more simple than getting on a horse and venturing no further than sixty miles from the center of town.

The *chagim* were over. It was September, a month when the signs of spring first appear, a month not too difficult for traveling. I purchased whatever provisions I thought necessary for the trip, and, having bid Rachel, the twins, and little Sarah farewell, I made my way west of the city at a leisurely pace.

For two days I traveled, content to take my time and grow used to the ways of the bush once again. My plan was simple. I was going to bypass George Matthews' old property, not by the regular route but via the hills that surrounded his property to the south. I would then work my way out from there in search of the aboriginal tribe we'd befriended a few years earlier, in the hope that they could help me with my quest.

On the third day out I recall coming to the top of a hill which gave me a beautiful view of the entire Western District. From there I detected the movements of a man. He couldn't see me as I watched him through my telescope, a gift given to me by Asher Hart. Perhaps this was Yankel Meisels.

Through my telescope lenses I watched the noticeably tired frame of the traveler leading a laden horse. As he came closer, I discerned him to be a very old man, thus ruling out the possibility of his being Meisels. He was extraordinarily thin, and his cheekbones protruded through the wisps of his white beard. Scattered locks of hair fell over his shoulders. A long jacket hung loosely on his emaciated frame. Yet as he approached me, I detected an uncanny, steady sparkle in his eyes. They were young and wise eyes, eyes used to gazing across the wind-hazed plains as they did now.

He leaned forward and watched a herd of kangaroos kick up dust as they swiftly hopped off into the bush. He then made his way over the narrow, rocky hill in front of him. He descended nimbly, placing his feet in the safest spots to avoid slipping. Now he waited, watching a thin train of clouds head across the sky. At last he climbed onto the saddle of his horse and gently nudged it with his foot. It started forward at a slow pace. The traveler stared intently at the land open before him. His haggard and worn face looked calm and peaceful.

What I didn't know at the time was that this was John Dunlop, the septuagenarian, on his way to Ballarat. He was looking for gold.

As for me, not only couldn't I find any evidence of white settlement, but I found no trace of the aboriginal tribe I thought would help me.

I had left on a Sunday. I didn't want to spend Shabbos in the bush, so I made my way back into town on the next Friday, to spend a quiet Shabbos with my family. Sunday morning I was out in the bush again. This time I decided to drop by Matthews' old property. Two hours out of Melbourne I rode through the rusty gates, which whined as they swung in the breeze.

There was nothing to be found there. The place was littered with decay. The wooden shacks had rotted beyond repair, the fences that had once possessed Matthews were broken in hundreds of places, and wild dogs called dingoes roamed in packs. There was only one thing of interest there and that was the state of what used to be Matthews' rooms. There was no doubt in my mind that the rooms had been recently occupied, though by whom was anyone's guess.

Employing some of the tactics that the aboriginals had taught me years earlier, I tried my best to follow any trails that led out of the property. I circled the station, closely checking every inch of earth. Yet, lacking the perspicacity of the aboriginal trackers, I was more than likely trampling over all the vital clues waiting to be read. But I did have one bit of luck. There was one set of horse tracks leading out in a southwesterly direction. Though I was not too wise on the subject, they looked relatively new to me—that is, they were clear enough to easily discern.

I followed them in the hope that they would lead me somewhere. Somehow I had the feeling that I'd find someone out there, although I wasn't sure whether that someone was going to be Yankel Meisels.

Late the next day, I made camp near a river. I washed and then collected twigs to make a fire. Once it was burning, I took a tin can, filled it with water, and balanced it on top of the fire to boil water for tea. After davening Maariv I sat down to eat supper.

The night was silent and clear. The full moon shone so brightly that, together with the stars, which were incredibly numerous and close, one might have had mild success in trying to read a book under the sky. I listened to the sounds of the night, reveling in its peacefulness. For the first time in my life, I realized how great an effect the bush had on me. I never felt so relaxed in my life. The only thing missing was my family.

I was halfway through my meal of salted meat and

bread when a quiet voice shot out of the dark.

"Don't finish it all off, Moses. I haven't eaten today."

As I heard a man's voice, I froze in fear, but before the sentence ended I realized who was addressing me. It was none other than George Matthews.

He laughed aloud, having derived immense pleasure in frightening the living daylights out of me. His laughter traveled across the night plains.

"What on earth are you doing out here, my good man?" he asked.

"I came all the way out from Melbourne just to be scared out of my skin by you," I replied.

"I've been watching you since last Tuesday. I thought I'd leave my entrance for an appropriate moment," he chuckled. "You're obviously looking for someone. It couldn't be that mad Dunlop fellow, because you saw him the other day and didn't make contact with him."

"Who?"

"That elderly gentleman you surveyed through that telescope of yours. He's out this way looking for gold. You aren't looking for me, are you?"

"No," I answered. "I'm looking for a man by the name of Yankel Meisels."

"Who?" he said, bewildered.

"Someone in England is looking for him. He is supposedly out here somewhere."

"These parts are deserted except for you, me, and old Dunlop."

"Forget Meisels," I said, changing the subject.

"What about you? You haven't been heard of in years. You simply disappeared off the face of the earth. What on earth for, I still don't know."

"I have my ways," he answered. "You might call me a bit of a loner."

"What have you been doing all this time?" I asked.

"Living out in the wild by myself and with the aboriginals. I've become quite adept at being able to roam through these parts undetected. It's been very interesting, actually. How is your family?" he asked, changing the topic as quickly as I had.

When I told him of the addition of our little Sarah, he was deeply moved. In the light of the fire, I thought I detected a look of lonely sadness in his eyes. I looked at him carefully. He hadn't changed much. He still carried himself well, his dress characteristically neat. I guessed he'd made a few trips into town to buy clothes.

His attitude towards me was that of an equal. We seemed to strike the note we'd left off at. I asked him about the property, and he told me that it meant nothing to him. He occasionally returned there out of habit, nothing more.

When I told him Asher Hart had purchased the remainder of his livestock from me and opened an account in his name, he broke into fits of uncontrollable laughter. Such an honest action in so crooked a world was, he termed, "completely out of character with the true nature of the colony." To him it was all a matter of hilarity.

As we turned in that night I had the uncomfortable

feeling that just as he had appeared out of nowhere, so he would disappear in much the same way. I told him so, adding that I wished to spend a couple of days with him. He readily agreed to my request and promised not to disappoint me.

"Why don't we have some fun," he said, "by following old Dunlop's tracks to see what he's up to. Maybe he's found the pot of gold he's looking for. And wouldn't it be amusing if he has!"

Chapter 14

The first thing I saw when I opened my eyes the following morning was Matthews sitting on his haunches staring at me. In that passing moment, I detected the same look of loneliness I'd seen on his face the night before. I got out from underneath my bedding, washed myself, and started to daven. I daven slowly, usually taking an hour to complete Shacharis, and throughout that time Matthews' eyes never left me. As I finished and was folding my *tallis,* he turned from me and started walking away from our campsite. He disappeared behind some dense shrub and a couple of minutes later emerged leading the same brown mare that he rode out on a couple of years earlier.

We ate silently and by seven-thirty were moving westward in search of John Dunlop. Matthews' bush sense was nothing less than remarkable, and I observed it in awe. He saw things that I hardly noticed, things like a broken branch, a faint impression on the ground, and the smallest droppings of horse manure. He told me that he had spent more than a year living with the aboriginals and, apart from their lack of sanitation, had found it a gratifying learning experience. During his sojourn with them, he told me, they were once set upon by a group of white men who would have massacred them all had it not been for Matthews' presence.

"There's no doubt in my mind that they were looking for blood. I'll never forget the looks on their faces," he said. "They were at once bewildered, shocked, and disgusted to find me living among men they considered nothing more than animals."

"Weren't you concerned for your life?" I asked.

"There were four of them. Three of them were easily persuaded. The mere sight of a white man, someone they could identify with, made them think twice. The fourth fellow was a giant of a man who called himself 'Wild Jack.' He would have taken pleasure in leaving me in a shallow grave. I could see in his eyes that he was itching to spill some blood, but the friendly attitude his friends took towards me made him feel uncomfortable."

"It wasn't Jack O'Hearn, was it?"

"Yes," he answered. "It was the same Jack O'Hearn who sailed the *Havring* with you."

He told me that the incident had taken place only a month before. O'Hearn's gang had afterwards gone to Melbourne, but for all he knew they could have returned to the area again.

"Wild Jack O'Hearn would be pleased to see us both

lying in our graves," I mused.

"Over my dead body," replied Matthews, breaking into his unique laughter.

By one in the afternoon we'd come to the top of another in a long line of soft rising hills. Matthews squinted across the plains at something not visible to my eye.

"Take out your telescope and look out there," he said, pointing.

I opened the telescope and, looking in the direction of his pointing finger, I saw the same solitary traveler I'd noticed the week before.

"Dunlop?"

"The same," he replied.

"He looks in a hurry, wouldn't you think?" I said.

"Give me the glasses," asked Matthews. I handed them to him. "I'd say he's quite excited about something. I haven't bothered the old soul in a month. He's a funny chap, our Dunlop. Doesn't like people encroaching on his territory. But old John doesn't have a say in the matter because he's about to be paid a visit by Mr. Matthews and Mr. Lazar, whether he cares for our company or not."

We rode down onto the open plain, circling around to approach Dunlop from the front, for fear, as Matthews thoughtfully put it, "of giving old Johnny a shock."

"Good afternoon, Mr. Dunlop," greeted Matthews.

"It is, indeed," he answered. "Is this man a friend?" he asked, cautiously eyeing me.

"He is both a friend and a gentleman," laughed

Matthews. "You're in a rush, I see," he continued.

"I must get to Melbourne quickly," came his reply.

"On what business?" he asked.

"The business of history, Mr. Matthews."

"What type of history are you referring to, sir?" I interjected.

Dunlop reined in his horse, For a short moment I could see a look of worry in his eyes.

"Can I trust you both?" he asked.

"You shan't find two more trustworthy men from here to Melbourne," said Matthews.

"Then promise me that you won't run ahead of me and break the news before I get to Melbourne."

"Break what news?" I asked.

"That there's more gold lying across the Ballarat plains than could fill the bank of England. Look for yourselves if you don't believe me."

At this he brought his horse to a halt and pulled open his saddlebags. To our amazement we saw that they were full of rich, yellow gold. There were nuggets the size of sovereigns and small, neatly tied bags of gold dust.

Both Matthews' jaw and mine had dropped so low at the sight that one would have thought our mouths were permanently positioned so. Dunlop's hands were shaking with excitement. He slapped the pouches closed, satisfied that we'd looked long enough at the contents.

"I'll be off then! But first your word," he said.

"You have it," replied Matthews. I seconded the promise.

"Only a word of advice before you go," suggested Matthews. "Don't take the direct route to Melbourne. You might run into a rather unkind ruffian by the name of Jack O'Hearn. I can think of no one more inclined to part you from your gold. You're too peaceful a man to have to waste your time with such a sort."

"Then how should I proceed?"

Matthews pointed out the safest route for old man Dunlop to take. He took leave of us immediately. We sat in our saddles watching him urge his horse forward. He hadn't left our sight when Matthews turned to me and asked me the obvious question.

"Shall we check out the gold situation ourselves or wait for the hordes to beat us to it?"

"When do you expect them to be out this way?" I asked.

"Give or take two days and the entire area from Ballarat to Melbourne will be full of men with greedy eyes bulging out of their sockets."

It was Tuesday. I had promised my wife that I'd return before Shabbos. That gave me more than ample time to ride to Ballarat with Matthews and satisfy my curiosity. I couldn't stay longer in the bush, as Rachel's family were due the following week and she'd need my help. I hadn't forgotten the purpose of my mission, to find Meisels, and yet, I reasoned, he could just as well be in the direction of Ballarat as anywhere else in the bush. Why not combine a search for the missing man—with a search for gold!

It was early afternoon and I would be lying if I said

that we weren't as excited as old John Dunlop. Both of us sensed that the luck that had befallen the old man would soon come our way.

When people think of gold rushes, they conjure up visions of fields covered by deep mine shafts and men descending and surfacing from them all day long like a colony of ants. This is actually the crux of the matter of mining. Once the gold lying on the surface is exhausted, the earth has to be broken and mined in order to extract its hidden treasures.

When the gold rush in Ballarat began, the first finds were indeed the nuggets lying on the surface of the ground or just below it. Nuggets were found under inches of loose earth, locked between blades of grass and scrub, and even caught in wedges at the bottom of tree trunks. Now don't think that these unexplored plains were covered with gold just lying around like clumps of grass. One had to search for the precious ore. This was painstaking work, but the gold was there, ripe for the picking, if one had the patience to look for it.

George Matthews and I were not miners in any sense of the word. When we left John Dunlop that afternoon, we had no idea of the extent of the gold deposits. We had no tools to help us dig, and really did not expect to be able to collect much gold. So you can imagine our sheer amazement at the vista that lay before our eyes as we rode into Ballarat late that afternoon.

The gold lay scattered across the fields, in places actually visible to the naked eye. At first we didn't bother to pick it up, content to roam the fields. We set up camp in what was to become the heart of the goldfields and rested, waiting for the morning to come.

Matthews wasn't as overwhelmed by the gold as I was. He was used to wealth and had, so he told me, never lacked for anything in his life.

The next morning we began the pleasant task of picking the fruits of our find. We stuffed the gold into our saddlebags and, when they were full, into our pockets. Matthews knew of a place east of Ballarat, on the road back to Melbourne, where we could safely hide our gold so that we could return and pick more. I followed him at a frantic pace five miles eastward to what we termed our bank.

It was an ingeniously secure hiding place, a large cavity in a tree that couldn't be seen from the ground and could only be reached if one climbed to the height of three men. What made it totally secure was that there were no lower branches on which to find leverage to climb. An aboriginal tracker had shown Matthews the tree.

We placed our first deposit of gold in the cavity and returned to Ballarat by mid-morning. By late Wednesday afternoon we had made three trips to the tree. Our finds were so substantial that we had enough gold to fill three trousers' legs. I will never forget Matthews constantly yelling out to me, "Moses Lazar, what does it feel like to be the richest man in Melbourne?"

I wasn't quite sure how to answer him. I hardly gave the future a thought. We spent the entire day with our eyes glued to the ground, and I wasn't yet able to understand the ramifications of this unexpected development in my life.

It was late Wednesday night, after we'd made our fourth trip to the tree and had returned to Ballarat, that we heard the first sounds of men in the area. Dunlop had obviously made an impression in Melbourne, for by the following morning there were streams of men on horseback and on foot spread across the hills of Ballarat searching for gold.

With the coming of the miners, the finds on the surface were, as I have already mentioned, quickly exhausted. By late Thursday, Ballarat had been transformed from nothing more than an unexplored tract of land to a bustling, crowded tent city, populated by men from every walk of life milling together like the men of Babel.

Neither Matthews nor I were sufficiently greedy to spend the coming years adding to our newfound wealth by mining shafts deep into the earth. As far as I was concerned, Hashem had been good to me. I felt that had He wanted me to dig dangerous shafts, he would have sent me out to Ballarat only after Dunlop's famous announcement to the world. But He had other plans and had opened a large treasure chest for me, allowing me to take until my heart was content.

And so early on Friday morning, nearly two weeks after I'd been sent out by the synagogue board on an act of *chessed*, I was returning. I had failed to find any trace of Yankel Meisels, but, unbelievably, now possessed gold worth hundreds of thousands of pounds, gold enough to ensure that I wouldn't have to work another day for the rest of my life.

Come Friday morning, Matthews and I had much to talk about. For one, it was impossible to carry all the gold back to Melbourne on one trip alone. We agreed that the wisest course of action would be to return to Melbourne together without the gold and find the most profitable way of selling it, after which we would come to an agreement as to how we would split it.

We trusted one another totally. I had no fear whatsoever that Matthews would rush back into the bush and grab the gold for himself. Neither was I concerned about leaving it out there.

It all sounded so simple, so elementary in design, such child's play. We laughed about it all the way back to Melbourne.

And yet nothing could have been further from the truth. The following days started off on a promising note, with Rachel's family's arrival. But that aside, there was nothing to cheer about, for the month of October, 1852, proved to be the most terrifying, the most painful, and the start of the most trying period of my life.

Chapter 15

The find at Ballarat came close on the heels of the California gold rush, and people were similarly infected by the exotic charm of the yellow mineral. The atmosphere in the streets of Melbourne was electric. As the extent of the find became known, more and more people abandoned their homes and work places. Over the coming weeks and months, the lure of the goldfields was such that even well-established men and women could not control their greed and hurriedly packed their bags for the goldfields. The magnetism extended across the seas to England, the rest of Europe, and America, and many new immigrants came after hearing that fortunes were to be made in Australia.

Matthews and I parted company after arrival in Melbourne. I came home to find Rachel and the children waiting for her family in excited anticipation. Two of the synagogue board members were waiting for me there, and I told them of my failure in finding Yankel Meisels. To be perfectly honest, the board members weren't as interested in hearing about Meisels as they were about gold. Indeed, our interview consisted of nothing more than a discussion of the finds at Ballarat.

With all the commotion of my arrival, I hadn't a moment alone with Rachel. My family and I were finally able to spend some time together once Shabbos came in. Naturally, I didn't speak of the gold on our day of rest. After Shabbos, Rachel started to tidy up the house, making sure it was as spotless as her mother would like. There was nothing I could do to keep her still. I asked her to bring out some cake and to put up a kettle of water for tea. I told her that George Matthews would soon be joining us on important business and that I had some news to tell her that would please her very much.

It took her a moment to digest the fact that Matthews and I had found huge deposits of gold, enough to keep us well-to-do for the rest of our lives. When she did comprehend it, her jaw dropped, much as mine had done when I eyed the gold in Dunlop's saddlebags.

She was aroused from her state of happy shock by the twins, who came running into the room excitedly.

"Mr. Matthews is here!" said Yaakov, hardly able to contain himself. Despite his long absence, the children had recognized their friend immediately.

Matthews came into the sitting room. He was so pleased to see my family that one would have thought that he was actually related to us.

"Has Moses told you the news?" he asked Rachel.

"Yes," she answered. "I still can't believe that it's true."

"But it is, Mrs. Lazar. And if word were to get out as to its general whereabouts, every man in this colony would be climbing trees in search of it. That's why I've come tonight. We need to make our find secure. Once it is, you and your good family can settle down to a life of luxury."

"I don't think we'll show extravagance," said Rachel. "There's much to be said for the simple life."

"Never a truer word spoken," answered Matthews. "I'm sure you'll continue to live a life of modesty, but a little money never hurt anyone."

We sat up late that night deep in discussion, my wife weaving around us dusting and cleaning. The children would occasionally come in, and every time they did, I could see a light shine in Matthews' eye. As he was leaving, I was overcome by the urge to know more of my benefactor and friend.

I said to him, "George, you won't shy away if I ask you a personal question, will you?"

He instantly became defensive. "Please don't," he said.

"I'm sorry. Only I am sure that were you to be honest with me, you'd benefit. I'm a person you can trust. Our relationship is close, but you maintain a distance that you won't let me broach. I'm sorry if I hurt your feelings, but I honestly feel that you're hiding from the world and from yourself."

"Maybe I am. But I choose to be that way."

"What's your secret?" I pursued.

His eyes looked away from me. Perhaps I had pressed too far.

"My secret, if that's what you call it, is mine and shall remain so."

"Why not let it out?"

"I'm sorry, Moses, but I won't let you press further. Let's leave this conversation be."

"For another day?"

"Let's just leave the subject alone. We have too much to do together without placing stumbling blocks between us. Worrying about the business of gold will serve us better. I'll be back here as we discussed, a week from tomorrow morning. Good evening."

With that he walked out into the October night, leaving me standing by the door, no closer to a solution of the mystery that surrounded him.

As for the gold lying in the tree some sixty-five miles from Melbourne, Rachel and I decided to discuss the impact it would have on us only once I had safely returned to Melbourne with it.

And so it was that for one week we tried to put the thought of gold out of our minds. Rachel's family was arriving, so there was excitement enough for us anyway. Our job was to see the family settled in as comfortably as possible.

The journey had been difficult for Rachel's parents, but her sisters had coped well and seemed ready to make new starts in life. The elder sister, Mindel, was a quiet, reserved woman. The younger sister, Leah, was the opposite in nature. She was vivacious and full of vigor. There was little we could do to tie her to the house. She'd bounce out the door early in the morning, run around town investigating anything of interest, and return late in the afternoon bearing the news of the day. It was obvious to Rachel and myself that Leah would have to be watched carefully. The electricity of those days could sweep away anyone, a young Jewish woman newly arrived from England included.

One of the first things that Rachel's father wanted to know was how we were making a living. He was impressed by the success we'd had tailoring but was concerned about our welfare after the fire. Tales of hidden gold left him unmoved: he would wait to see with his own eyes the treasure I was to bring back with me. As far as my mother-in-law was concerned, she couldn't have cared less about the gold. The only thing that mattered were her grandchildren. How she doted on them! Her presence in our household brought about a significant change in our lives. Rachel was given a new lease on life and found enormous resources of untapped energy and strength. It was a joy to watch her and her mother spending their days together.

Mindel busied herself around the house, helping with the children. After three years in Australia, she met and married a young Jewish immigrant by the name of Rottenberg, a man dedicated to her. Having successfully sold merchandise of all kinds in the goldfields, he eventually took Mindel back to England, where they and their family still live.

But it was Leah who really thrived in the clear Melbourne air. The vast expanse in Australia suited her down to the ground. The town became her playground. Indeed, if I look back over the last fifteen years, I have to admit that it is Leah's story that first gave me the idea of writing down my life history.

The problem with Leah was simple: Possessed of a curious nature, she instinctively followed her path in life without considering the consequences of her actions. In England she had been surrounded by Jews, and whatever she did was done within the close-knit community of Stepney. But the moment she stepped off the ship in Melbourne, she felt free of the shackles that bound her to conformity. Only a few months after her arrival, Leah announced that she saw no necessity for being restricted by ancient laws that were out of place in Australia, where the number of Jews was too minimal for Yiddishkeit to be of real significance.

Her parents were horrified by her attitude, and it led to a break in their relationship which might have ended in tragedy.

But all this was yet to come. For now, my main concern was getting my newfound fortune safely back home.

Early in the morning, eight days after Matthews had paid us his nocturnal visit, I saddled my horse in preparation for the ride out towards Ballarat. I was to meet Matthews just outside Melbourne. We planned to ride out to Ballarat to observe the gold rush first hand. We would then make our way back to the tree, collect our gold, and return to Melbourne before Shabbos. Everything seemed simple and straightforward.

We rode along what once had been a lonely trail. Now traffic clattered along, men on horses or in carriages, others walking, all sharing the same purpose—to get to Ballarat and make their fortune. There was an air of camaraderie which came to be characteristic of the time. Greed might have blazed in the eyes of the prospectors, but the sweat and toil of digging bound them together in brotherhood. In any case, there was no need for jealousy: by the look of things there was no lack of gold at Ballarat. There was plenty to go around and satisfy those with enough determination to spend their time and energy looking for it.

Not every person coming to Ballarat came in search of gold. Many subsidiary businesses sprang up overnight as a result of the gold finds. Great fortunes could be made by opening up businesses. Some men became gold buyers and sellers, others shopkeepers or pub keepers. Of course, the prices of goods on the goldfields were much higher than in town. There was no lack of men anxious to part the miners from their newfound wealth. Not used to handling such vast sums of money, many men went on spending sprees. Most of the men in the fields never considered taking their money and depositing it in a bank or investing it in some enterprise. They spent it as fast as they could earn it. Famous stories abound of the newly rich lighting their pipes with paper money and buying huge crates of champagne, only to finish the contents within a matter of hours.

There were social changes as well. Convicts sent out to Australia like myself became rich overnight, and the divisions in social class structures began to disappear. Men who originated from the lowest rungs of life now had equal status with those men and women who, prior to the gold rush, were the only representatives of wealth in the colony.

These, then, are some of the things Matthews and I saw as we rode around Ballarat at the beginning of the gold rush.

It was late on Tuesday night, as I sat reading, that Matthews came crawling into our tent reeking of rum. I remembered how he freely admitted that he liked to drink during the time I spent working with him. I had forgotten about this vice of his and was shocked to see him in such a drunken state. He reeked of spirits, looked a shabby mess, and to make matters worse, was cursing as freely as a chimney spews forth smoke. I tried, unsuccessfully, to ignore him.

"Moses, Moses, Moses," he cried. "My dear Moses. Will you ever learn that you're too righteous for me?"

"Lie down, George," I said, taking his arm and guiding him to his bedding.

"Take your holy hands off me!" he shouted. "No! No! Moses Lazar, the good Jew that Georgie Matthews dragged off the *Havring*." He lost his balance and fell against the side of our tent. He thought this a matter of hilarity and spent a good minute in fits of laughter. Then he seemed to remember where he was and continued cursing me.

"I knew you were Jewish the moment I set eyes on you. I wanted to resist the temptation but couldn't let the good Jew pass by without giving him employment. Since then my conscience has weighed as heavily around my neck as a ball and chain."

"I'm sorry if I've played on your conscience," I said.

"You're sorry! Fool that I am, I gave you work. I'm to blame. I'm to blame. It's my fault." At this he began to weep. Through his sobs he continued on. "I brought it upon myself. If only I could escape from you and every Jew that existed. You haunted me in England and you haunt me here. When will I see the last face of the last Jew in my life? When?"

He was now crying uncontrollably. I watched him in pity. What a lonely creature, what a sad man, I thought to myself.

"I can't escape the God of the Jews. Why can't I escape God?" he cried. He repeated this last sentence over and over until he finally fell asleep some time later.

I was just finishing davening the next morning when Matthews awoke. He looked horribly hung over, but cheerful nonetheless. He washed and dressed and spoke in lively tones about the day that awaited us. Amazingly, he showed no signs of the previous night's happenings. When I told him that he'd been terribly drunk, he laughed aloud.

"I wish I knew what it is I do when I get drunk," he said.

If he wasn't giving away his secret when he was drunk, he surely wasn't going to when he was sober. His secret, so I thought, was so tightly locked away in his heart that it would take extraordinary circumstances to unleash it from him.

And extraordinary circumstances they were!

Chapter 16

We were in a jovial mood that Wednesday morning as we made our way out of Ballarat. The road taking us to our fortune was not long. The five miles would be quickly covered, and soon we'd be on our way back to Melbourne to live our lives in luxury.

We came to the point in the road where we were to turn left into the bush. The way was clear so we started off at a quick pace. We'd gone about three hundred yards when Matthews suddenly pulled his horse to a stop. I followed suit and watched as he dismounted, walked forward a few paces, and closely inspected the ground in front of him. He came back to where I waited.

"Someone passed through here yesterday. There are three horses. The tracks run in the direction of our tree."

"Do you think that someone has got wind of our find?" I asked.

"No. But we can't go down in that direction and hope that we won't be seen."

"What do you suggest?"

"Let's walk from here and scout around to see who's in there. They may be friendly, they may not. Then again, for all we know they may have ridden straight through here and not stopped."

We tied our horses to a strong tree and made our way forward on foot, with Matthews leading. He continually searched for signs on the ground and in the trees. For a mile we came across no one. Then we passed a campsite, its wood fire still smoldering. Walking further into the bush we came upon three horses tied to a tree. We crouched low among the bushes and waited.

We must have been there for only a few minutes when, like a bolt of lightning, a gun shot rang out through the bush. We heard the sound of galloping hooves coming towards us from the rear and, in a moment, a huge masked man high astride a black horse was upon us. He fired another shot and two men came scurrying out of the bush. They were upon us in an instant. Matthews was easy prey for them, but I fought hard and they had a difficult time pinning me down. The men backed away from me when the man on the horse fired another shot into the air.

He pulled down his mask. The face was none other than that of Jack O'Hearn. He laughed viciously.

"You'll let my men tie you up if you care for your life, Jew Lazar," he said.

I wasn't going to argue with him. I valued my life too much to have it taken from me by such an unworthy scoundrel. "Tighter," he shouted, not satisfied that his men were tying us properly.

The rope that was attached to our hands was tied to the saddle of O'Hearn's horse, and in this manner we walked back towards the main road. He brought us to the place where we'd left our horses, and then forced us onto the ground.

"What a surprise to find you out here, Lazar. And who would have thought to find the man who loves blacks with you," spoke O'Hearn.

"What do you want with us, O'Hearn?" I asked.

"Want? From you? Check their horses," he ordered one of his men. The man hurried to where our horses stood and rifled through the saddlebags. He returned quickly.

"Nothing there, Jack," he reported.

"What brings you two out this way?" O'Hearn asked.

Matthews was about to answer when I interjected. "What business is it of yours? We're free men going about our way. What right do you have asking us such questions?"

"No one answers Wild Jack O'Hearn like that," he said, as he spat at my feet. "I could shoot you now to shut your mouth."

"Why use weapons? Be a man and fight me with your bare hands," I answered.

"Not this time, Lazar. This time you'll stay where you are until the time's ripe."

"Ripe for what, O'Hearn?"

"Ripe to lay you and your friend here to rest in a shallow grave. Now, what are you doing out here?" he asked again.

"Minding our own business, which is more than I can say for you and this mob of yours," I challenged. "What, may I ask, are *you* doing out here?"

"We are about to start a small business whereby we relieve travelers of their belongings free of charge."

"You devil!" I said.

O'Hearn motioned to one of his men. The fellow came forward and made an attempt to hit me. I lifted my unbound feet hard and fast into the fellow's abdomen. The other one ran towards me and struggled with me until O'Hearn came down off his horse and clubbed me across the back of the neck with the butt of his pistol. I fell to the ground, groggy and in pain.

"Open your mouth again, Jew, and I'll use the other end of this pistol," he swore. Then, addressing Matthews, he repeated his question. Matthews answered that we'd come looking for gold.

"Why don't you go to Ballarat like the rest of them?" asked O'Hearn.

"We thought we'd try our luck in places no men had been," he answered.

O'Hearn seemed satisfied with Matthews' answer. Why shouldn't he have been? Everyone coming out this way was looking for gold and there was no reason to suspect us of doing otherwise.

O'Hearn posted one of his men to watch over us

with the strictest instructions to shoot if we did anything suspicious.

"I haven't forgotten our last meeting, Lazar. You're going to pay heavily for that. You'll wish you never crossed my path." He then rode off with the other thug of his, the man I'd kicked.

My head hurt terribly, but I had my senses about me. I was sitting with my back to a tree. The ropes that bound me were tied tightly. O'Hearn had told his men to do a good job on me, warning them that were I to break loose, they'd be taught a lesson they could ill afford to learn. Fools that they were, they did as they were instructed with me but didn't pay as much attention to the knots they used to bind Matthews. It wasn't long after we'd been tied that he motioned to me that it wouldn't be hard for him to wriggle himself loose. Though an escape attempt was risky, what was there to lose? O'Hearn was bloodthirsty enough to carry out his threat. Why wait around for him?

Over the course of an hour, Matthews managed to untie the ropes. He kept his hands behind his back, waiting for the right moment. The time passed slowly. The guard didn't always pay the strictest attention to his job, yawning occasionally out of boredom. Each time we saw an opportunity, we thought it better to wait until we were completely certain. Finally, the perfect chance arose.

The guard walked up to where Matthews was tied and squatted a few feet in front of him. He was being brave, cursing us at what he imagined to be a safe distance. He looked at Matthews and said, "You're a smart one, aren't you, black man? I ought to take my pistol out and finish you off right now."

"That would be impossible," Matthews answered.

"Why's that, man?" he asked.

"Because you're too much of a coward to do so."

"Oh, am I?"

"Look at you. If you were brave you'd come closer, and not keep yourself over there like a coward. Are you scared of a man tied to a tree?"

"I'm not scared of anyone!" he said defiantly. He approached Matthews. When he was no more than a foot or two away Matthews lunged at him with all his might. The man didn't know what hit him, and he was soon lying on the floor, arms and legs trussed up. Matthews then ran to me and untied me as fast as he could.

"Let's get out of here," I said. "I'd stay and wait for O'Hearn, teach him a lesson, but there's a chance one of us would get hurt, and that's a risk I'm not willing to take." I grabbed the guard's pistol. "Let's go!"

But as luck would have it, O'Hearn had heard the noise of the fracas and rushed back to see what had happened. He charged the two of us with his horse. I dodged to the side and grabbed the reins as the horse went past. O'Hearn tumbled to the ground. He wasn't injured and got to his feet quickly. I was about to tackle him when O'Hearn's other man rushed. This fellow was brave but was no match for me. I tried to bring the gun in my hand down hard on his head, but he thwarted the blow by blocking it with his arm. O'Hearn came from behind him and aimed his pistol. I grabbed O'Hearn's henchman and used him as a shield to stop O'Hearn from firing a shot at me. O'Hearn weaved this way and that trying to get a shot at me, but I wouldn't give him the opportunity.

This entire time Matthews had been standing dumbstruck a few yards behind us. O'Hearn's man fought in an effort to escape my grip. He succeeded, and then there was nothing between me and O'Hearn.

He pointed his gun at me and fired. I heard a cry ring out behind me. O'Hearn had missed me but had shot his henchman, who clutched his chest and dropped to the ground. My gun was loaded. In a wild rage I pointed it towards O'Hearn, who had reloaded his gun, but just as I did Matthews inexplicably came between us, his back towards me.

I cannot recall whether I heard two or three shots. I felt a sharp pain in my arm, and my head started spinning. All I remember seeing as I collapsed was Matthews falling forward on his face and O'Hearn bent over in agony.

Chapter 17

Daylight was just breaking through as I regained consciousness. I tried to rise. The ground was cold and I wondered why I had so much of it in my mouth. Then I remembered where I was. I made an attempt to get to my feet and felt again the excruciating pain in my right arm, where the flesh was torn away. The bleeding, at least, had stopped.

Try as I might, I couldn't find any trace of the melee. The area didn't look familiar. Perhaps, I theorized, I had staggered away after being hit.

I walked around in a daze for some time, until I came across two fresh, shallow graves. With my left hand I scraped away at them. After much effort I discovered that Jack O'Hearn lay in one and his accomplice whom he'd accidentally shot in the other. I covered them over again and sat down next to a tree to think. The only person who would have bothered to dig these graves was O'Hearn's other man.

What, then, of George Matthews? I searched for him for over an hour. I managed to locate the place where we'd fought, but there was no trace of him anywhere. I then walked back to where we'd left our horses. My horse was there, but Matthews' horse had vanished.

I got on my horse and went off in search of Matthews. It must have been about nine o'clock in the morning when I came upon O'Hearn's other man, the one Matthews had beaten. He was lying semiconscious on his back in a pool of blood. When I dismounted and stood above him, he looked at me bitterly.

"Is there anything I can do for you?" I asked.

"Just leave me to die in peace," he replied.

"Who shot you?" I enquired.

"Your friend," he answered.

"Is he alive?"

"He was dying when he left me," said the fellow.

"What happened after the fight?" I asked.

The fellow took a shallow breath and spoke.

"I managed to get untied and ran in the direction of the gunshots. I found O'Hearn and Carrigan dead. Your friend, too, was lying still on the ground. I was sure that he, too, was dead. As for you, I took some time in finding you. You were some sixty yards away. I noticed that you were still breathing. I hated you then as I hate you now and decided to finish you off, but not before I had buried O'Hearn and Carrigan.

"I dug two graves and buried them. I then took my pistol and started to walk in your direction but as I cocked it and pointed it at you, your friend rolled over and shot me from where he was lying. I guess you can say that he saved your life."

"Was he hurt?" I asked.

"He was shot through the back," came the reply.

I shuddered when he said that because it could only have been me who had shot him accidentally.

"What then?" I pressed. The man's face paled. He had trouble speaking but I pressed him. I had to know what had happened.

"Your friend pulled himself up, and came to where I lay. He looked at you and must have thought you were dead. He began to dig you a grave but the pain in his back was such that he gave up after a few minutes. He pulled himself up on his horse and rode off, slumped over in the saddle. I'd say he was going the same way I'm going now. He'll be dead before you find him."

The man started gasping for air. I had nothing to give him and watched helplessly as he lost consciousness. I must have fallen unconscious again, and by the time I awoke, he was dead.

I got on my horse to look for some sign of Matthews. For hours I searched the area. Just as I was giving up hope, I came across his horse. It was riderless and covered in blood. Had he fallen off? Again I searched fruitlessly until nightfall. By that time I hadn't an ounce of energy left in me. I tied the two horses together, washed myself down as best as I could, took out some bedding, and tried to daven Maariv as I lay there. I managed to say *Shema* and fell fast asleep.

The following morning I awoke feeling somewhat better. I spent much of the morning looking for Matthews, but in vain. What had happened to him? From all accounts he was dead, for who could survive a gunshot wound in the back? I had accidentally killed him. I felt horrid. I felt like a murderer.

What was I to do? Stay out in the bush and continue the search, or return to Melbourne without finding his body? What about the gold? Was it better to leave it where it was or load it onto my horses and take it back to town?

After sitting on the damp ground for hours deep in reflection, I decided that the best course of action to take would be to collect the gold and then go back to Melbourne to recuperate. Once I had regained my strength, I would come out again and find Matthews' body.

I led the horses to the hiding place. When I arrived, I realized that a superhuman effort would be needed to climb the tree. I could barely extend my right arm, thus making it virtually impossible to find the leverage necessary. I positioned the tallest horse below the tree and stood on the saddle. My left arm just reached the edge of the cavity. With all my remaining strength, I pulled myself up until I was balanced on the edge of the hole in the tree.

I saw the bags of gold lying inside, untouched since the day we had deposited them there. I lifted each bag and threw it to the ground. By the time the cavity was empty, I felt dizzy and nauseated. I sat up in the tree waiting for my strength to return so that I could descend. Jumping onto the horse seemed dangerous because there was only a little space to land on, so I jumped directly onto the hard ground instead. I fell spreadeagled across the bags and lay there, once again waiting for my strength to return. Finally, I loaded the bags onto the horses and began the journey back to Melbourne.

It was Friday morning when I started off. Usually such a trip would take four hours at a medium pace, this time it took me longer than six hours. I arrived some time before Shabbos, half dead from exhaustion.

I don't remember much about that Shabbos other than the look on my wife's face as I pulled up outside our house. I gave a few orders for the bags to be safely stored away, alighted from my horse, walked into the house, stood at the edge of my bed, and collapsed onto it.

By the time I had regained sense of myself, it was early Sunday morning. The pain in my right arm was sharp and my head ached. I noticed that I'd been bathed and bandaged. The questions that were directed to me by my family were many, but the answers they received were few. I was in no mood to talk to anyone. I had lapsed into severe depression. It was the first time in my life that I felt so full of despair.

When I was feeling somewhat better, Rachel came to my bedside holding a document written in Matthews' hand. It detailed the directions of how we were to invest the gold that we'd found. Rachel pointed out to me that she wasn't prepared to have a fortune's worth of gold lying idly around the house. Could she carry out the instructions of the letter or not, she asked me. I nodded that she could. She then sent the children out to fetch Asher Hart and his cousin Henri. She told the astonished men of our newfound wealth. They read through the document and promised to fulfill its instructions to the last word.

Originally the plan was to divide the gold in half between Matthews and myself. As he was probably dead, nearly all the gold was transferred into money and deposited into a bank account under my name. A fairly large portion of the gold was stored away in the house. A few days later, Melbourne's leading banker informed us that we had nearly one hundred thousand pounds deposited in my name. So much for being one of the wealthiest men in Melbourne. Frankly, I couldn't have cared less. I lay in bed for a week recuperating. Apart from the flesh wound on my right arm which was healing quickly, I had suffered from shock and what the doctor termed "overexposure to the elements."

Though my body began to heal, my depression deepened day by day. It was bad enough to know that Matthews had died a terrible death, but to think that I had shot him in the back, the man who had saved my life many times over, was all too much to bear. I didn't know how to deal with such a situation. I prayed to God, begging Him for forgiveness and the strength to manage. I thought the situation through as rationally as I could, but with no sense of relief. I forced myself to speak to my wife and to Rabbi Rintel, but no matter what I did, I spiraled further into despair.

Rabbi Rintel was wonderfully sympathetic and did his best to give me comfort. I had been trying to save my life, which was my obligation as a Jew. In doing so I had shot a friend. Matthews' death had been a tragic accident, and I should not hold myself responsible. The fact that I had survived such an ordeal was a miracle that I was obligated to recognize.

"Hashem," said the rabbi, "has need for you in this world. He rules it so completely that what you experienced was obviously meant to be."

As for the conversations that took place between Rachel and I, I can only say that I should have listened to her. Her common sense far outweighed my stubbornness.

In retrospect, I wish I had taken heed of the advice both she and the rabbi gave me. They counseled me to thank Hashem for my life, to mourn for my lost friend, and to continue my life as a Jew. Their good advice, though, went unheeded.

I sat at home for two weeks. When I'd had enough of the house, I went for walks which took me all over Melbourne. I wandered around like a lost soul, hands buried in my pockets, my head sunk low on my chest. There were days when I'd be out from morning to late at night. All I saw in my mind's eye was Matthews' face smiling at me. It haunted me every moment of the day. I'd wake up more than a dozen times at night, bathed in a cold sweat, suffering from nightmares which invariably relived those dreadful moments in the bush.

These nightmares then took on a new twist. Awoken by them, I'd lie in bed, fully conscious, still seeing the images before my eyes. Rachel would hear my shouts and on more than one occasion said to me, "Moses, it's all right. You're only dreaming."

"I know I'm dreaming," I answered her, "but the nightmares persist even when I am awake."

Nothing consoled me, no words, no deeds, no gestures. In my eyes I was a murderer. The remainder of my life would be spent carrying a burden of guilt on my shoulders. I didn't feel that I was built strong enough to withstand such a weight.

My outlook on life deteriorated as quickly as my bodily health returned. It was like moving from one sickness to another.

After a month, I felt myself strong enough to venture out into the bush to look for Matthews' body. The idea became an obsession with me. Despite my wife's objections, I started making preparations, and in late November, 1852, I once again traveled into the bush. I spent a month out there in the heat of the summer sun and never once found a trace of my dear friend, George Matthews. I returned empty-handed to Melbourne, a dejected, miserable man.

Had it not been for Matthews, I used to muse, who knows where I might have ended up. He took me off the *Havring* and gave me the chance to earn my freedom. I was indebted to him. Despite his faults in my eyes, he was a righteous gentile. I would miss him dearly and forever wish that I had never pulled the trigger that ended his life. He had left this world saving my life in a situation where he could have saved his own.

I rapidly fell into deeper depressions. Happiness, as I had once known it, no longer existed for me. I suffered terribly, causing my family no end of sorrow.

And all this after having become one of the richest men in the English colony of Australia.

Chapter 18

For two months I continued to roam the streets, leaving home early in the morning and not returning until after dark. I ate little and spoke less. I had withdrawn from the world and from those I loved. I had literally cut myself off from everyone. I felt like a man caged, locked behind a door without a key.

Rachel watched me anxiously and, when she saw my mood grow darker with each passing day, finally resolved to take action.

One hot February morning, she took a large portion of the gold that we had kept in our home, wrapped it carefully in a plain piece of cloth, and took it to a local goldsmith, an honest man whose talents were perfectly suited to the age of wild gold rush fever. Rachel can be both mysterious and direct when the need arises. She bid Mr. Cobden, the goldsmith, good morning and laconically said she wished him to forge something for her. She gently placed the cloth on the table before him. He opened it and tipped its contents out onto the felt tablecloth. Then he stared, stunned.

"Mrs. Lazar," he said. "I cannot recall seeing such a large quantity of gold as this before." Retelling this story many years later, my wife told me how she sat mute as he let the pieces of gold run through his fingers. "Mrs. Lazar, this is most extraordinary. What do you wish made? Necklaces, rings, a plate?"

"This is what I want commissioned," she answered. She placed a small lithograph on the table next to the piles of gold.

Mr. Cobden held it up to the light. "Why, Mrs. Lazar, this is most unusual. Do you mean a copy of this?"

Mr. Cobden then contemplated the print, looking at it intently.

"Quite a task," he whispered.

"You'll do it, then?" asked Rachel.

"Why not? It poses a challenge that I've rarely faced in my work. Certainly more exciting than necklaces and the like."

"It's for my husband. I need it quickly. His health depends on it," said Rachel nervously.

"I will do my utmost, Mrs. Lazar. Come back in a fortnight."

Meanwhile, I was still suffering. I couldn't concentrate on my prayers and found going to the synagogue a burden. Rabbi Rintel tried giving me counsel. We spoke for hours on end. Once again he emphasized to me that as a Jew I was obligated to accept what Hashem had planned for me. Moreover, I didn't deserve to punish myself in such a masochistic manner. I needed to trust in Hashem. He, and only He, would see me out of my malaise.

"I cannot believe that a man like you is acting this way," he said. "After all you experienced and overcame on the seas from England, you are allowing yourself to lose faith in Hashem, to lose all that you have fought for until now."

He was right, of course. One could see what I was becoming. I put on *tefillin* perfunctorily, I said kiddush over wine on Shabbos with no feeling, I attended classes with the rabbi with no conviction or concentration whatsoever. I couldn't cool my blood to body temperature: it still seethed with guilt.

I paid cursory attention to my family and watched like a distant observer as my wife's family settled into Australian life. Her parents enjoyed the quiet of Melbourne. My wife had seen to it that we moved into a large, beautiful house, partially for the sake of her parents.

Out of great respect for my wife, I must say that having such vast sums of money at her fingertips never distorted her outlook on life, which remained (and still remains today) solidly rooted in her devotion to the simple ways of Yiddishkeit and the basic things in life. If anything, her access to money only increased her will to extend her hand to those in need. The house she chose to move into was large because it had to house our family and the constant stream of Jewish immigrants who came to us as their first port of call after disembarkation.

My wife's sister Mindel stayed at home and helped around the house. She cared little for the bustle of the city. Leah, however, kept herself busy and was rarely at home. The freedom of a new country found her romping freely from one part of town to the next.

In a way, we were similar, Leah and I, in that we both left the house at the same time in the morning with nowhere in particular to go. But the similarity ended there. She raced through life as if there was no tomorrow. It was as if she was in a rush to get somewhere fast, afraid that she might never arrive. As for me, I was busily attempting to escape life. Both of us seemed to be making good progress towards our undefined goals.

Living in Melbourne in the early 1850s was akin to watching a caterpillar turn into a butterfly. The city rapidly changed in character. The pace of life quickened from a canter to a gallop and the excitement could be felt in the air. It was a dangerous time, a dangerous place for a young girl easily influenced by external forces.

Leah went through a dramatic and rebellious change in life. She fought her parents tenaciously every time they caught her walking out the door. They cajoled, they threatened, they even tried locking her indoors. The only thing that did work, albeit temporarily, was warning her that should she continue wandering about town, she'd be sent back to England.

In my depressed state, I was in no mood for a

recalcitrant sister-in-law. I was short with her, and she had no patience for me. She often complained to Rachel that having been convicted and sent out to Australia had irreparably changed me for the worse. Rachel tried to make her understand that the loss of George Matthews had come as a terrible blow to me. Still Leah and I drifted further and further apart from one another, and it wasn't long before we stopped acknowledging each other at all.

Once we came to a sharp exchange of words. I was walking back home one evening and decided to take a longer route than usual. I had just jumped a fence and hadn't taken more than five paces along the dirt road when I saw Leah deep in conversation with a group of young men and women. What struck me most was that I'd seen one of the men before. He was a free immigrant from England who, at a glance, looked respectable enough. I, however, had several times seen him drunk as a man can get, using the most despicable language imaginable. Leah, I thought to myself, would better serve herself keeping company with young women of good character. It is true that there weren't many Jewish women to keep company with, but anything was better than the types I saw on the road that evening.

"Come along with me, Leah," I said, as I approached the group.

"Whatever do you mean, Moses?" she answered at a loss.

"Your parents are waiting for you at home," I said.

"And who are you to set an example?" she snapped

back in fury. "My sister's been waiting for you every day for the last two months, so don't lecture me!"

I was dumbfounded. I stood there in the middle of the road as she walked away with her friends, all of them laughing and joking as they went. Our exchange had only taken a moment, but its effect on me was enormous. First, I was shocked by her attitude. It frightened me that such a young woman could have such a sharp tongue. My mind projected to the future and a shudder ran through my bones when I thought about her. She was following a course that was to bring her sorrow sooner or later.

The second point that I couldn't keep out of my mind was how right she had been when she castigated me. George Matthews or not, my wife was obviously suffering from my absence. I recalled the *parshah* of *Tazria* and how appropriate it was in my situation. A person who has become impure must go through a process of cleansing in order to return to his household in a pure state. When a person is impure, it is as if a part of the *shechinah* has left him, and a person who doesn't have the *shechinah* resting upon him is not a complete Jew. The same lesson can be applied in my case. Having fallen into a fit of uncontrolled melancholy, it was as if part of the *shechinah* had left me. I was an incomplete Jew needing purification.

I didn't immediately recognize this second point. At the time I was still smarting from Leah's insolence. The seeds of what she had said took a long time to root but at least they had been planted. My road to recovery had begun.

Oh, but what a road back! In my madness I acted like a complete fool. I decided that I was not worthy of the gold I had found. I blamed the gold for Matthews' death. The fortune I had made sat safely in the bank earning a handsome rate of interest. I thought that I could rid myself of it by being reckless.

Word travels fast in a small colony and news of my wealth spread like wildfire. Apart from the poor who came for money, to whom my wife gladly gave as much as was needed, men of business approached me for counsel and money, usually with the purpose of asking for investment in some promising project or another.

Roaming around as I did, you might think I was hard to find, but the opposite was true. I was like the pollen on a flower sought out by bees. Bankers, merchants, businessmen, and conniving swindlers all showed remarkable wit and perseverance in finding me. If it was on a street corner, under a tree, or at the port, they swarmed around me, only too willing to milk me of my fortune.

At first I ran from them, not wanting to deal with anyone. Then I got the idea that were I to invest money in the most ridiculous of projects, the ones I thought least likely to succeed, I would easily lose the money in no time and thus rid myself of the heavy burden of guilt as well. Also, I thought it a wonderful form of amusement. So I let them seek me out where they would and the only condition I made for myself was that I wouldn't do business with respectable types, men who had made their marks in the world as successful merchants or bankers.

It was to the most unlikely to succeed that I turned my attention. Within a matter of one month I had become partners in the most ridiculous projects of folly imaginable. Some of them failed, of course, like the one hundred pounds I handed over to a serious young man, who, having served his seven year term of service to the Queen, wished to purchase some land and start a small farm. I readily became a partner in his scheme. Not a week had passed when he disappeared with the money. Three other men disappeared with similar amounts.

Yet my plan did not work out as I'd foreseen. I became a partner to one Arthur Bishop, a middle-aged immigrant who was convinced that a general store in the middle of the goldfields would make a fortune. I thought his idea hopeless. Miners, I believed, were make-do men who carried their every need with them. What's more, I didn't believe that the gold rush would last forever. So I signed the legal papers with Mr. Bishop and provided him with enough money to build a store and supply it with a miner's every need. I insisted upon the best, most expensive store that we could build. In all, I handed him over three hundred pounds.

Bishop couldn't believe his luck. For that matter, neither could I, when he returned a few months later handing me over triple the original amount. He had struck it rich and was to provide me with a large sum of money every month for over three years.

A few months later, I was approached by Mr. Howard Crompton, who came to me with a plan of buying up small businesses in the heart of Melbourne that were increasingly being abandoned as men went in search of gold. I was sure we'd lose on such dealings, reasoning that perhaps the vast deposits of gold out there were, indeed, inexhaustible. Melbourne, I reckoned, would eventually become secondary to larger towns situated around the goldfields. Years later, after the gold rush waned, my investment in this business, totaling over a thousand pounds, multiplied so many times, that it alone was worth more money than my initial find with Matthews.

I succeeded when I wished to fail. I made fortunes when I wanted to lose them. This one came wanting money to start a delivery service between Melbourne and Sydney. Another sought to finance a small fleet of ships. Two others wanted to buy a thousand head of sheep and herd them northwards through unchartered territory to rich grazing lands which were also up for sale.

And all these wild plans bore fruit. They transformed me from a rich man to one of the wealthiest men in the colony. Some thought me lucky, others swore I was brilliant, whilst I, fool that I was, slowly came to the realization that I was stuck with good fortune, and nothing petty or foolish I could do was likely to change my position in life.

It was in this way that I spent my time in pursuit of financial failure, and found, instead, inescapable success.

Chapter 19

Who knows how long my madness would have persisted? Though Leah's sharp words had stung, and I resolved to be more attentive to Rachel's needs and more congenial to her family, I still was locked in the deathly grip of guilt and melancholy. But Hashem, in His mercy, once again sent my beloved helpmate to lead me out of the darkness.

One morning, some months after I'd embarked upon my foolish course of ridding myself of my wealth, my wife greeted me with a mysterious smile. She led me into our spacious kitchen and gestured towards a large wooden box on the table.

"I've a present for you, Moses," she said softly, pointing to the box. "Open it!"

I sat at the table and lifted the top off the box. Inside, nestled against a lining of straw, was the most beautiful menorah I had ever seen. I sat speechless.

"I took the liberty of having this forged out of some of the gold you found," said Rachel.

"But why?" I replied, dazzled by the light as it glistened off the menorah.

My wife smiled. "To teach you a lesson."

"I don't understand," I said, looking at her.

"Look at this menorah, Moses. See how the gold you discovered can be molded into something so beautiful, something you will use to glorify Hashem's name. Gold and money are not evil in themselves—it all depends on what use they are put to.

"I remember," she continued, "Rabbi Rintel once spoke of the menorah that was lit in the Temple. It was a symbol, he said, of our gratitude to and appreciation for Hashem. He does so much for us—so we do what little we can for Him, and light the menorah.

"Hashem watched over you on the *Havring*, did not abandon you in this wilderness, saved you from O'Hearn, and made you a wealthy man besides. And where is your gratitude to Him, Moses? Where is your gratitude?"

The rays of the morning sun came through the window, striking the shining beauty of the gold. It was as though its light had penetrated the darkness that had enveloped me for so many months.

I silently vowed that I would heed my wife's wise words. And I kept my vow: from that day forward, I did my all to become a good husband, father, and servant of Hashem. Though the thought of Matthews still pained me, I left melancholy and guilt behind.

With this bleak era of my life over, I hoped for a life of peace and serenity, but alas, it was not to be. Shortly after I had changed my own disastrous course, another tragedy befell our family.

After our encounter, I had avoided Leah's presence. To be honest, I felt uncomfortable with my sister-in-law, and hardly knew what to say to her.

One morning, the family awoke to find Leah's room empty. She had left nothing more than a small note saying she was off in search of greater adventures than Melbourne could provide, and that rather than be threatened with banishment to England, she was going to live her life as she, and no one else, saw fit.

Her parents and sisters were frantic and we made every effort to find her. We tried everything we could, visited every known haunt of hers, asked anyone and everyone, and placed advertisements in the local newspaper. All this led us nowhere.

Days and weeks passed and not a word was heard from or about Leah. Her parents were literally in mourning. Our household was in shambles. Yet somehow the family had a feeling that Leah was alive and well. She was a tough, adventurous sort who had never once in her life submitted to hardship. This feeling, however, offered little solace.

Freed from the burden of earning a living, I spent my time trying to comfort my wife and her family and searching for Leah. I found solace only in my daily lessons with Rabbi Rintel. I spent most of my day in the rabbi's small office, making use of his library to increase my Torah learning. My thirst for knowledge knew no bounds. I felt that I had discovered the reason why I had become so wealthy. As a rich man, there was nothing to interrupt my course of Torah study. Yet my ideal in life was not to last. It seemed that the Almighty was not yet content with my new learning program. He had one more adventure planned for me.

Though personally I felt a serenity that I had never felt before, I could not bear to see my family's sorrow. I looked at my mother-in-law's red-rimmed eyes, my father-in-law's gaunt face, and knew that I had to do something.

After days of deep thought, I reached a cataclysmic decision: I would go into the bush, risk hardships once again, and try to find my errant sister-in-law! My first stop would be the goldfields, the natural destination of a young girl in search of adventure. I would find Leah, and would bring her home!

My decision both horrified Rachel and, after some time, filled her with hope. Of course, she longed to find her sister, and yet she feared that the rigors of a bush journey would bring me to harm.

But I wasn't interested in objections in any case. My decision reached, I wished to set out without delay.

At the back of the stables in a small, windowless room that reeked of stale air, I found all the provisions I had once put to good use on my journeys into the bush. Piece by piece I began throwing them out into the morning air. As I did, a ripple of excitement ran down my back—the feeling of adventure overtook me once again.

Chapter 20

The next few days were spent in frantic preparation. Rachel and the twins helped me put together parcels of salted meat, dried fruits, and fresh vegetables. The children found pleasure in playing with every bag, rope, and instrument that I was trying my best to organize. By noon Thursday I was ready to leave, but, as I had done on my previous journeys, I decided to wait until after Shabbos.

With nothing more pressing to do, I spent the remainder of the day playing with the children. It was five o'clock in the afternoon when Rachel got up to answer a knock at the door. I listened as she opened it. I heard a few words, but could distinguish nothing. Then I heard her shouting in excitement, "Moses, come quickly. Moses!" I walked to the door, where I saw her standing, her eyes sparkling, a letter in her hand.

"Who was that?" I asked.

"He said he just arrived from Ballarat. He brought us wonderful news."

"Who's it from?"

She handed the letter to me. It was Leah's handwriting. I read it aloud. "I am well. Engaged to marry. Arriving Thursday 19th. Leah."

"Very strange," said Rachel, rereading the letter.

"Yes. It doesn't give any indication of where she's been or who her fiancé is," I agreed. "When is Thursday the 19th?"

"One week from today," said Rachel. "Thank God this came when it did; now there's no need for you to go into the bush. You know how much I hate your leaving us."

"I'll admit I'm relieved myself," I said.

Apart from the food parcels, I didn't bother to unpack the bags I'd prepared for my journey. True, I was happy to get back to my learning, yet the thrill of adventure had come and gone without my saddling the horses. In a way I felt cheated and so decided to wait a few days, until my excitement had waned, before unpacking.

Early the following Sunday morning, as I was making my way to Rabbi Rintel's study, I noticed a carriage with its shutters drawn pass me. A few hundred yards on I watched as it turned around and made its way back in my direction. As it drove past me again I saw the curtains move slightly. I couldn't see the face within and, with my mind on other things, I continued on my way not giving the carriage or its occupants a thought.

I spent the day deep in learning and, after sunset,

began to make my way home. I had totally forgotten about the carriage that had mysteriously passed me that morning and so was surprised to see it head towards me once again. It looked a bit sinister and aroused my curiosity. Who was it that was so interested in my person?

It was an expensive carriage, drawn by two powerful horses. If I made any effort to chase it, I would be outrun, so there was no question of making a dash at it. I pretended not to notice it as it passed, but when it did, I ran into the road behind it and lifted myself up onto the back of the carriage. The coachman made no sign that he suspected anything.

A couple of hundred yards along the road the carriage turned around, then halted. I heard a knock coming from the cabin. A muffled voice called out, "What are you waiting for, man?"

"Can't see him, sir. Seems to have taken a different route," called out the coachman in reply.

"Well, find him!" came a shout from within. "Where could he be?"

Just before the coachman whipped his horses, I got down off the back of the carriage, came around the side, opened the door and got in. By the light of a small lantern I saw a small, wiry man of thirty-odd covered by a black cape.

"Where could who be?" I said, sitting opposite him. The man gazed calmly at me, as though my entrance had no effect on him whatsoever. "It is me you're looking for, isn't it?" I asked.

"Who are you?" he asked nonchalantly.

"I thought you knew," I said. My tone became cold. "I'm not used to being followed around by a coach with its curtains drawn. You had better tell me who you are or you'll be sorry you ever set sight on me."

"Sorry!? Hah!" His staccato reply echoed in the small space of the cabin. "If you're who I think you are, my friend, welcome."

I stared at him for a long while trying to calculate my next response. He stared back defiantly. The features of his face were sharp. His crooked nose didn't fit the rest of his face and I assumed that it had been broken and left to mend without proper medical guidance. His eyes were cautious and beady. His whole countenance was that of a man who is not to be trusted. I decided to let him lead me where he would, all the while keeping on my guard.

"My name's Lazar. Am I the man you're looking for?"

"As a matter of fact, you are," he answered.

"Well," I said, "speak your business and be quick about it. I'm a busy man."

"You'll be busier." He rolled out the last word as though he were singing it slowly: bi-zee-er.

"Are you going to tell me what this is all about or not?" I asked impatiently.

"Am I trying you a little, Mr. Lazar?" he asked condescendingly.

He was running the conversation around in circles, toying with me. I didn't need to suffer such nonsense.

"You're not trying me in the slightest. You've just

taken up too much of my time. Good day," I said. I opened the door to the carriage, jumped down on the road, and walked away.

The man with the crooked nose leaned out of the window and laughed aloud. I hadn't walked more than ten paces when he yelled after me, "George Matthews will be disappointed!"

I stopped in my tracks, turned around towards the carriage, and watched as the man's face contorted in laughter. He infuriated me.

"Do come back inside, Mr. Lazar."

I did his bidding and climbed into the now stationary carriage, curious to hear more from him.

"You dare throw George Matthews' name around like that and I'll take immense pleasure in throwing you around," I warned him. "Who are you trying to impress, riding around the streets like this? If you wish to speak to me, knock on my door. Don't follow me around the streets as if there's a price on my head."

The man cowered a little in his seat. His grin had vanished. I wasn't finished with him, though, and I yelled at the top of my voice, "Speak!"

"Patience, Mr. Lazar," he timidly replied. But after a moment or two he reassumed his air of authority. After all, he had information he sensed I wanted. "I've been sent to find you."

"By whom?"

"George Matthews."

"He's dead," I said.

"He's not. He's alive and in need of your company."

"How do you know him?" I asked.

"I was returning from Ballarat last week when I came across him."

"Was he alone?"

"There were some blacks with him. I didn't see anyone else."

"He's dead!" I said again. "I saw him shot."

"He didn't look in complete health," continued the man. "You can argue with me all you like, Mr. Lazar, but the man claimed he was George Matthews. He awaits your arrival. I'll be more than pleased to give you a ride out there."

"Give me proof," I said, still not totally convinced of the man's sincerity.

The fellow dug into a pocket underneath his cape and pulled out an envelope. The seal had been broken. Before I looked at the contents, I said to him, "You've either forged this or broken the seal. Which is it?" The man showed little embarrassment. "No guessing at that question, is there?" I grumbled.

I took the paper from inside the envelope. It was written in Matthews's inimitable handwriting. It read:

"Fruitful trees bear long friendships. If you have plucked the fruit of the tree I have no fear that it is as safe as the love I have for you. Please come to the property. George Matthews, former employer and partner."

"There's no date on this. Why did you open it? How do I know that you haven't had this in your pocket for months?" I asked.

"One question at a time, Mr. Lazar. Firstly, I've had it since last week. As to opening it up, I might have taken that liberty. I didn't want to feel as if my search for you was in vain."

"Nonsense," I retorted. "You probably hoped this letter might reveal some valuable information. I suppose you tried hard to decipher this?"

"It makes little sense to me. Matthews told me I'd have no luck, but I tried anyway."

"Do you have any other matters to discuss with me?" I asked.

"No," he answered. "You might pay me for my services."

"What services? Following me like a bloodhound or delivering the letter," I said cynically.

"Let's just say that I've kept you entertained," he replied.

"Come to me next Sunday afternoon and I'll give you five pounds. I'll be back from Matthews' property by then." He made signs of a weak protest but before he could say more, I had slipped from the carriage and was on my way back home.

"The ride, Mr. Lazar? My carriage is at your service. Can I take you home, or maybe out to Mr. Matthews' property?" he called to me.

"Next Sunday afternoon!" I shouted back.

"Very well, then," he answered. With that, the carriage made its way up the street and turned left. I felt relieved to see it gone.

On my way home I weighed everything up. The

writing looked like Matthews' and the note made sense enough. What was there to lose? There was nothing more to do other than find out for myself whether it was George Matthews who waited for me. My horses needed no packing and my food was prepared. The following morning, soon after daybreak, I was on the road, westward again.

Chapter 21

I was excited about the possibility of seeing my friend George again, but I was nervous as well. I didn't know what to expect. Was it really George Matthews, alive? Was he very ill? And did he bear me any rancor? After all, he'd been felled by my bullet!

My eyes saw little of the road, except to note an increase of travelers. Soon I turned off the main way and continued on over those beautiful undulating hills, under the familiar richness of an Australian sky.

I paused momentarily when I came to the top of the hill overlooking the property. I recalled the first time I had stopped there, the day I stepped off the *Havring*. Matthews had lectured me about hard work and his need for a firm foreman. Those few moments brought back memories of the time I brought my wife and children off the boat, of Darcy, Masters, and young Coulhoun playing with the children. It reminded me of the sheep and of the land, but most of all, of Matthews. I gently applied pressure to my horse, and she slowly cantered down the hill towards the rusty gate.

From the front gate to the shacks, all was in shambles. The place appeared abandoned. Then I saw him. He was a shadow of his former self, but it was George Matthews. He had come to the doorway and was standing there, leaning against the rotting frame. I rode up to the shack and looked at him.

"Good day, Mr. Matthews."

His grin widened. "I never thought you'd get here," he said.

"Here I am. At your service," I announced, bowing in my saddle.

"Despicable creature, wasn't he?" he said.

"Who?"

"The one I sent to find you?" he declared.

"Oh, him," I laughed.

"Yes. A contemptible, ignominious wretch would better sum him up, wouldn't you think?" he added.

"Do you have any adjectives left?" I asked.

"Yes," he said. "I look horrible but I feel wonderful and am delighted to see you. Do get off your horse and shake a man's hand." I got off my horse, took his hand, and then gave him a hug which made him yell out,

"I didn't know you were so happy to see me. Come in, I must lay down."

I followed him inside. If the outside of the shack looked as if it was ready to cave in, it gave no clue to the room itself. It was spotless. A few books were piled on a chest of drawers. The bed was neatly covered with a quilt. On the floor lay a woven rug and in the corner rested a chair to which he pointed me.

He lay on the bed. I looked at him again. He had lost a lot of weight. His clothes hung loosely about him and he had aged a good deal, but he was still full of cheerful spirits.

"I thought you were dead," I said, picking up the conversation.

"Did you? I thought you were dead," he echoed. His eyes wandered to a point somewhere above my head and he kept them there as if transfixed. "Do you remember much about what happened?" he asked, his eyes resting on me again.

"Just your coming between O'Hearn and me and then hearing two or three shots. I fell with a wound in my upper arm. When I regained consciousness, I looked for you. Finally I came across one of O'Hearn's men, who was dying. He said you saved my life. That's all I know. I've walked around all this time thinking I killed you. I've practically been in mourning."

"That's very noble of you, Moses," he said. "I, too, remember coming between you and O'Hearn and hearing shots."

"What made you do that?" I interrupted.

"A moment of insanity, I suppose. I felt a pain in my back which could only have come from your pistol. You must have killed O'Hearn with the same bullet because my pistol jammed stuck. Your shot knocked me out for a while and when I awoke the pain was unbearable. As I lay on my side bleeding, I was certain that my last day on earth had come. I thought you were dead. I watched one of O'Hearn's men come to take a shot at you, out of spite I guess, and with all my energy I twisted my body far enough to shoot him. It was lucky for you that my pistol didn't jam again.

"I wanted to bury you but hadn't the strength. Instead I used my last ounce of energy to climb on my horse. I pointed it in the direction of an aboriginal tribe I knew. They found me before I found them. They are primitive and have practically no knowledge of medicine, but they cleaned my wounds as best as they could and left the rest to the Almighty, as you would say. They nearly killed me when they decided it was in my best interest to travel north. They dragged my horse and me for three days until we finally came to a thick forest where they let me rest in what I can only describe as a very comfortable cave."

"Now I understand why I couldn't find you. I finally gave you up for dead," I said.

"And me you. I'm lucky I'm alive, Moses. I was hit in the back just below my shoulder blade. Anyway, after three months or so I had enough strength to ride my horse. I came back looking for you but there wasn't a trace of the incident to be found. I decided to stay in the bush indefinitely, but we came into contact with white people, some of whom were from Melbourne, and it was through them that I heard that you were alive and well."

We sat in silence for a few minutes.

"What are your plans?" I finally asked.

"Why, I'm going to come back to Melbourne with you. I'll stay overnight. Then I wish to be taken to a hotel where I will stay until I recover. After I have regained the necessary strength, I shall come to a decision where to live and what to do."

"Nonsense!" I appealed. "You'll stay with us."

"Thank you ever so much," he said, "but I'd prefer it my way."

"As you wish," I said. "As far as money is concerned, you'll have no problems. I can heartily assure you of that. Your money has unexpectedly grown in value over the last few months," I laughed.

"A successful speculator, Mr. Lazar?"

"A lucky fool would better describe me," I replied, embarrassed.

"I never had any doubts about trusting you with my half of the share."

"After you've settled down, I would highly recommend your marrying. You need a wife to look after you. You can't live in the bush forever."

"Oh, I don't know. I have time to sort myself out. I might do a number of things."

"It's three o'clock. I don't mind waiting until tomorrow morning, but I'd be happier to return to Melbourne now, if you didn't mind. Do you have any objections?" I asked.

"None. You'll find my horse none the worse for wear in the stable. All I wish to take with me are those books and whatever is in the drawers at the end of this bed."

"You stay where you are and I'll arrange everything," I ordered. "I'll call you when we're ready to leave."

Less than an hour later, we were on our way back to Melbourne, our two horses gently trotting alongside one another. We spoke little on the way back, more content to bask in the peaceful silence that rested between us. It was not until we reached the outskirts of the town that we began talking. He was interested to hear about my family. When I mentioned the children his eyes lit up. I also told him of my wife's parents and sisters. Then I related to him Leah's disappearance, and her surprising letter.

"She says she's engaged to a fellow. I'm only guessing, but I think it may be that Meisels fellow I once came out your way looking for."

"Would your sister-in-law marry someone who isn't of your faith?" he inquired.

"I'd like to think not," I replied. "She wouldn't send us a letter stating she was about to marry if he wasn't a Jew. She knows that her parents have read it, and should the fellow not be Jewish, she is not foolish enough to think that they would accept it peacefully."

"How interesting," he said. "You Jews are a funny lot. Do you mean to say that if her man was an honorable one, but not a Jew, they wouldn't accept the marriage?"

"It's a great crime for a Jew to commit," I said. "It's a deadly course for assimilation." We cantered on in silence for a few moments.

"And here, Mr. Matthews," I said, pointing to the brown picket fence, "is my house."

"Goodness me!" he exclaimed. "Where on earth did you get the money to buy that? Did it fall out of a tree?" We both broke into laughter and this brought the family outside. Greetings were exchanged all around.

Having heard so much about him, my parents-in-law peppered him with questions, and this tried his strength somewhat. Finally, I drew him a hot bath, which he sat in for over an hour. Then, refusing any supper, he went directly to bed.

Matthews ate a hearty breakfast the following morning. I accompanied him into town, where he purchased an entire wardrobe for himself. Then, ignoring my protests, he insisted I take him to Melbourne's most respectable hotel. Rachel sent enough assorted foodstuffs to him in the hotel to keep him satiated for a month.

We spent most of that week together. I took leave of him late Thursday afternoon. I promised to drop in for a visit soon after Shabbos. He told me he would be away for several days, and that he'd come to see me as soon as he returned. He refused to give me a hint of what business was taking him out of Melbourne.

I recall parting from him at the entrance to the hotel, his right hand held above his head in salute. As I made my way back home that day, I never thought that it would be the last time I would ever see George Matthews as I'd come to know and love him.

Chapter 22

As expected, Leah arrived late on Thursday. She bounced off the horse drawn carriage that had brought her into Melbourne with typical self-assurance. She kissed her parents and the rest of the family and even went so far as to smile in my direction. Then, as we were still gathered around her, she announced, "I'm getting married one week from Sunday at three o'clock in the afternoon, so please don't go making other arrangements. It would be so awkward if you did."

"My Leah," cried her mother. "What has become of you?"

"Don't look so shocked, Mother. And don't worry, he's Jewish through and through."

"Thank God for such mercies," responded her mother.

"Who is he?" asked her father.

"It wouldn't be a certain Yankel Meisels, by any chance?" I questioned her.

"Have you been following me around?" she asked me. "How did you know who my husband-to-be is?"

"It was a guess," I answered.

"Why the secrecy?" asked Rachel.

"There are no secrets. His name is Yankel Meisels, as Moses has stated."

"Can't the wedding wait a few weeks so that we can organize a fitting function?" asked Rachel.

"No," she declared. "I've waited long enough for this day. I will marry next Sunday! Let's go home. I'm so tired and hungry."

"Let's," I said in reply. "I only have one question to ask you before we go."

"And what is that, Moses?"

"It's the obvious question. The only one to ask, in fact," I said. "Your future husband, Mr. Yankel Meisels, where is he?"

"His plans are such that he won't be able to arrive in Melbourne until next Sunday. He'll be here in time for the *chuppah*, don't worry. I'll tell you all about my adventures when we get home."

We collected her baggage and went on our way.

In the warmth of our kitchen, we eagerly crowded around Leah and listened as she unraveled her tale. She had, she freely admitted, run away from home. Life in a Torah-observant household seemed restrictive to her, particularly in the vastness and freedom of an unexplored land. She had visions, she admitted with a self-deprecating laugh, of a new, better, more exciting world. And so, on a whim, she'd traveled to the goldfields.

When she came to Ballarat, she was overwhelmed by the atmosphere of mud, gold, drink, and avarice. Was this the freedom she was seeking? She'd been in Ballarat for less than a month and had grown quite disgusted with its rowdy, hedonistic life. If this was life without restrictions, she wanted no part of it! She decided she'd return to Melbourne, to her parents, and to her Jewish way of life.

One night before her planned departure, she overheard two men discussing some aboriginals they'd met some thirty-five miles outside the town. What interested Leah most was their description of a white man whom they claimed—they weren't sure about it—they had seen lying inside a flimsy tent.

Leah immediately thought of the story of the missing Yankel Meisels. Perhaps this was the missing Jew! Ashamed of her hasty actions and repenting the sorrow she realized she'd caused, Leah wondered if she could possibly bring some good out of evil. She vowed to see if she could aid a sick man, possibly a Jew.

The next day she hired a horse and wagon and drove off in search of the tribe. After circling the outskirts of Ballarat all day, she finally came upon their encampment. The aboriginals were friendly, clearly used to contact with white men, though rather astonished to see a woman so far out in the bush. In reply to her questions, they took Leah to a tent, opened the flap, and revealed what lay within: the emaciated gaunt figure of a white man. They gave his name as Yankel Meisels. It was the missing man!

Leah returned to Ballarat that night without speaking to the sleeping Meisels, but she came back early the next morning and, without a word, began to nurse the sick man back to health.

Meisels stubbornly refused Leah's repeated requests to seek medication in Ballarat or Melbourne. Apart from his claim that he was too weak to travel, he simply didn't seem to care about living. He revealed nothing to her of his past, claiming he'd left nothing but a string of litter behind him, a wasted life of emptiness. Some days he refused to speak at all, and instead sat and stared ahead of him at the endless bush.

Leah ignored his surly behavior. Each morning she would appear out of the mist, tend to the man, cook his meals, and speak to him when he cared to listen. Then, before the sun set, she'd ride back to Ballarat, where she locked herself in her hotel room.

The days turned into weeks. The man slowly succumbed to his better instincts and began acting like a gentleman towards Leah. He told her the truth about his past. She convinced him to move into Ballarat, and he reluctantly agreed to do so.

By the time he had regained his strength and spirits, Meisels proposed to Leah, who assented. Leah then sent off the telegram to her family and preceded Meisels to Melbourne.

With Leah's return the atmosphere in the house changed drastically. Her parents, listless since her disappearance, were rejuvenated. Laughter emanated from every room. Our children were wild with excitement, and

Rachel and I were carried away by the joy of the impending *simchah*.

The sounds of the *zemiros* that livened our Shabbos table hadn't been heard in too long a time. It was as if we were singing as hard as we could to make up for all the silent Shabbosim we'd spent over the previous months. Leah sat at the middle of the table beaming with pride.

In her eagerness, Leah hadn't considered some of the more basic aspects of the marriage ceremony. There was only one hitch that Rabbi Rintel, who would act as *mesader kiddushin*, could see—the necessity of Yankel Meisels proving that he was Jewish. The glint of confidence left Leah's eyes. Concerned, she asked what procedure had to be taken should her *chasan* lack the necessary papers. The rabbi answered that witnesses would need to be sent for. In short, she might have to bear a wait of some time. This unnerved Leah, who had thought the ceremony was just a matter of course.

So she was a bundle of nerves on that Sunday, her wedding day. We spent the morning in frantic preparation. The children spent most of the time running to the windows, hoping to catch sight of Leah's fiancé. Morning became afternoon and, as the minutes disappeared, so did Leah's patience. At two-thirty we left for the synagogue, and her husband-to-be still hadn't materialized.

The wedding guests, which included most of Melbourne's Jewish population, milled around the center of the synagogue, expressing their opinions of the extraordinary events that had led to this hasty marriage. The wedding was scheduled for three o'clock. At ten to three Leah was beginning to lose hope. At five to three her normally bright eyes were full of tears. Then, at exactly three o'clock, a shout went out from one of the congregants.

"There's a carriage pulling up. Could that be him?"

Leah rushed towards the windows facing the street. She let out a cry, "He's here!" Leah made her way over to a large wicker chair where the *chasan* was to stand over her and cover her face with the beautifully embroidered white veil she was wearing.

Rabbi Rintel, holding the *kesubah* that still needed completion, walked slowly towards the door. There was total silence. Except for the footsteps of the approaching groom on the path outside, not a sound could be heard. He came to the door and slowly turned the handle. He walked into the packed synagogue with a sea of anxious faces staring at him.

"Good afternoon," he said. "I do apologize if I'm late."

There, in front of us, stood Leah's *chasan*—George Matthews!

At first I refused to believe my eyes. My mother-in-law fainted, my father-in-law had to be restrained, and I was in a near state of shock.

"Oh, Yankel! I thought you'd never come," cried Leah.

George Matthews, my former employee, partner, and friend stood inside the door of the synagogue looking quite overcome by the proceedings going on around him.

"Would someone please explain to me the meaning of this?" said Rabbi Rintel. "Who are you, sir?" he asked, addressing the groom. "Are you Yankel Meisels, as I assume you are supposed to be, or are you George Matthews? The matter is crucial if you have the slightest intention of marrying this woman according to the law of Israel."

"I am both George Matthews and Yankel Meisels," responded the groom. The congregants began talking among themselves and Rabbi Rintel, collecting himself, asked the prospective groom and bride, her father, and me to step into his office.

Walking into the rabbi's room, I had a sinking feeling in my heart. My mind was quickly trying to explore the possible scenarios for the bizarre events of the afternoon. If this was the George Matthews I knew, then Leah couldn't marry him because he wasn't Jewish. If, on the other hand, he was really Yankel Meisels as he claimed, then witnesses would have to be produced to prove his assertion. These two scenarios were straightforward enough.

But a third, more problematic, possibility entered my head. What if Leah, having traveled out into the bush, had found George Matthews and fallen in love with him? How, then, could they manage to arrange a marriage that appeased her parents? George had known about my failed journey out to find Yankel Meisels. Perhaps he calculated that Yankel Meisels would never be found and that he could safely acquire his identity, thus finding a means to marry Leah.

We sat around the table in Rabbi Rintel's office. The Rabbi looked most perturbed.

"Sir," he said, addressing the groom. "We must establish who you are. You are known to me only as the non-Jew, George Matthews. Should you wish to marry this woman, you will have to produce evidence proving that you are Jewish. Is that understood?"

"It is," replied the groom.

"George, who are you?" I interjected.

"I'm as Jewish as you, Moses," he said.

"Yankel, would you please prove who you are to the rabbi," said Leah.

"Yes, young man, prove who you are before you give my wife another bad turn," added Leah's father.

We all looked expectantly at the *chasan* waiting for him to furnish the proof we all demanded.

"Well sir? We're waiting," said the rabbi impatiently.

"Rabbi," he said, "as Moses well knows, I have spent the last months in ill health. When I finally returned to my property I found that it had been ransacked and vandalized. All that remained were a few books, some bed coverings, and some money I hid for a rainy day. Gone forever, stolen, I'm afraid, are the documents that prove I'm Jewish. However," he said, "I am as Jewish as anyone in this room.

"I was born Yankel Shmuel Meisels and was raised in the north of England. I have spent the last eight years in this country under an alias."

"For what reason?" asked the rabbi.

"While still in England, my attachment to my

Jewishness began to wane. I left the customs of my parents and my parents' parents. My family might not be as observant as you, sir, or Moses beside me, but I became a disgrace to them nevertheless. Nothing they did would convince me to repent my ways. I was belligerent and caused them much grief. I admit my actions went too far. I acted defiantly one Yom Kippur and disgraced my family. I then decided to exile myself from England and start a new life.

"I came out to Australia and for a while I was completely happy. However, as time went on I found that there was something in my soul that yearned for attachment to the ways I had been brought up with. Hence my employing Moses. I knew he was Jewish the moment I set eyes on him. True, he is taller than most Jews I've known, but there was something about him that instinctively told me that he was a Jew.

"As long as he was in my employ, I felt as if I was fulfilling the barest minimum necessary for a Jew to perform. I had attached myself to the Jewishness of my past without having to practice it. I lived vicariously through Moses' righteousness. If not that, at least I was fulfilling an important commandment by giving him and his family fair employment and good living conditions under my roof.

"My family, may God strengthen them, finally heard that I was in this colony and made enquiries, which, coincidentally enough, sent Moses here on a wild goose chase through the hills looking for Yankel Meisels. The irony of all this was that I was with him most of the time.

We had luck and found gold together but unfortunately ran into trouble. As you know, we were involved in a gun battle and both of us assumed the other dead.

"When Leah found me in the bush, weak and sick, I introduced myself to her as Yankel Meisels because by then I had seen God's hand in everything I'd done and had decided to repent my ways. She helped nurse me to health and we decided to marry. We set a date, but rather than make myself known beforehand, I chose to make the dramatic entrance that you have all witnessed."

"You tell quite a tale, sir," said the rabbi, looking perplexed. "But stories don't satisfy our demands. We need something more concrete than your life history."

"I'll be the first to drag you under the *chuppah* if you are who you say you are," I told him. "Isn't there anything else you can give us?"

The groom, until now confident that his story was enough, was starting to look a trifle shaky.

"I thought I had another avenue, but that seems to have failed," he said.

"What is that?" I asked.

"What difference does it make? I can't provide you with what you need."

"Write to your family. They'll send the documents," said Leah's father hopefully.

"I have done as much, but the documents, if they sent them at all, are more than likely on the high seas."

A gloomy silence fell upon the small room. Rabbi Rintel looked at me in sympathy, hinting that he believed the story but was at a loss what to do.

The silence was interrupted by a commotion in the synagogue. The sounds of a scuffle just outside the door broke out. I walked to the door to investigate. When I opened it a man fell on his face at my feet.

"The audacity of the man! Says he's owed five pounds," blurted out one of the congregants.

"Did everything we could to keep the fiend from entering your office, rabbi," said another.

I pulled at the man's shoulder and turned him over. To my astonishment it was none other than the scheming little fellow who had mysteriously pursued me a week earlier. He got to his feet and straightened his clothing. When Matthews saw who it was he got to his feet and walked briskly towards him.

"Well," he said. "Did you find him?"

"I do believe you owe me money, sir," he ranted. "And you, too," he said, looking at me.

"You'll get your money, man, but more importantly, did you find him?"

"Yes, I did," he answered. "He's outside waiting in the carriage."

The groom ran from the room and through the throng of onlookers standing at the door.

"What, in God's good name, is going on?" asked the rabbi.

"I think we'd all like to know," I said.

Moments later, the *chasan* came panting back into the room. He was followed by an elderly gentleman. I offered the gentleman my chair, which he accepted with a gruff thank you. His face was familiar—surely, I thought, he was the gentleman who had cursed Matthews so long ago on Cashmore's Corner. I emptied my pockets, which contained some six or seven pounds, and handed the money over to Matthews' messenger, whose name we never came nor cared to know. When he realized that the sum in his hand was more than he had bargained for, he bowed low in appreciation and disappeared.

The rabbi continued his investigation as soon as the door to his office was closed.

"And who, sir, might you be?" asked the rabbi.

"Who might I be? The temerity of it all. I think it better that I avoid this scoundrel," the old man said, pointing in the groom's direction.

"I'm terribly sorry," said the rabbi. "I do apologize for your discomfort. Do you recognize this man?"

"I most certainly do!" he bellowed. This last comment quite amused the groom, who broke into that familiar laugh of his. The old man turned on him in a fury. "You ought to be beaten, Jack Meisels. If I were twenty years younger I'd give you a proper hiding. And I'd do it in the name of your good parents. What anguish and sorrow you've heaped upon your family! What utter despair they've lived through."

"Excuse me sir," interrupted the rabbi, "but what name did you call this gentleman by?"

"Yankel Meisels is his name. Known to his friends in England as Jack."

"Could you prove that the man sitting here is Yankel, or Jack Meisels, as you call him?"

"Why? What's he calling himself this week? You can run to the far corners of this earth, Meisels, but no matter where it is you will never be able to escape what and who you are."

The groom's voice was suave. "Mr. Kahan. My dear Mr. Kahan. You have stepped into my life at a most appropriate moment. Indeed, you will agree with me that you, of all the people in this colony, are the one person I usually would most benefit by avoiding. Why is it then, do you think, that I sent out a man to find you? Obviously, sir, you must agree that matters have changed somewhat in my life for me to want to confront you. No?"

"I believe we are all owed an explanation," said Leah's father, who, like the rest of us, was completely at sea.

"Please do it quickly, Yankel. I want to get married and I don't intend waiting around all afternoon," echoed Leah.

"It would give me the greatest of pleasure to do so," said the groom.

The last piece of this strange puzzle was about fall into place. But before the groom had a chance to go any further, there came another knock on the door. One of the wedding guests stepped into the room wanting to know whether the wedding was going to go ahead as planned. The rabbi stepped outside and asked the guests to have a little more patience, stating that his investigation was nearly at an end.

He reentered the room, closed the door behind him, sat down behind his desk, and motioned to the groom to continue his story.

Chapter 23

"My name is Yankel Meisels, not George Matthews. I took the name Matthews for myself when I came to Australia nearly eight years ago. Men who change their names often do so out of fear. They run across the world to flee their pursuers. I suppose for most men this is an effective way of starting a new life.

"My story runs on similar lines. I have been running away from my past for years. My belief was that, by sailing out to Australia, a land relatively unknown to civilization, I could start a new life.

"What was I running from? I was running away from the law brought down from Mount Sinai by our greatest prophet, Moses. Unlike other men, though, I found it impossible to escape from Yiddishkeit. I could refrain from keeping the mitzvahs, but my conscience wouldn't bear the weight of my decision.

"I have always respected my parents, but their traditional Jewish way of life was too demanding, too rigid, and too restricting for me. By the age of twenty-three I had tasted enough of life outside my parent's home to want to taste more. I couldn't hide this from my parents, and the ensuing years found us at odds with each other. I left to live in London, but wherever I went, I felt entrapped by their will. Finally, the pressure became too much for me, and nearly eight years ago, I sailed out here.

"Upon arrival I convinced myself that I had extinguished the fire of Judaism from my soul. Initially I found the spirit of adventure exciting enough to take my mind away from such matters. Yet as the years progressed, I came to realize that the embers still burnt. They singed my conscience until I could no longer exist without the taste of Yiddishkeit in my soul.

"I was on the verge of writing a letter of apology to my parents. I even considered returning to England, when, looking for a worker on the docks of Melbourne, I came across Moses here. To my bewilderment I discovered that he was most observant in his ways. I say bewilderment because I felt as if struck by a blow. It was as if God had sent him to me with the express purpose of reforming me. You might say it was a challenge between God and myself.

"I believed I could fulfill some form of vicarious obligation through Moses. This worked for a while, although I must say there were times when I was tempted to return to Judaism. Just watching how Moses acted towards his fellow men was nearly enough to convince me that I should repent. For didn't all of Moses' actions stem from his understanding of what God wanted from us? Somehow, I was always able to persuade myself otherwise, concluding that living vicariously was a perfectly honorable existence. At times, however, when I was sure my better will was about to overpower me and find me confessing to Moses, I escaped by working hard during the day, thus taking my mind off the matter, or drinking spirits at night until I was totally drunk. I admit that there is nothing more ignoble than drink. It only served as a means to an end, an escape from reality.

"Why didn't I fire Moses to rid myself of my conscience? It was because he had become a part of me. To rid myself of him would have been perilous, for it would have been akin to killing a portion of my own self. I wasn't foolish enough to abandon the one tie I had to Yiddishkeit, because I finally realized that I needed to remain attached, somehow.

"All this changed after Moses and I were involved in the shooting accident you are all aware of. I nearly died from a gunshot wound inflicted accidentally by Moses himself. He believed me dead and I believed him dead. Throughout my sickness I had much time to reflect about my past. I struggled against death and disease, but struggled harder against my conscience. It was during these tortured months that I saw the hand of God. I felt Him tugging and pushing at me, urging me to repent. I saw the depths of disgrace I had taken myself to. If I dreamed, I dreamed about my childhood.

In these dreams I saw my parents, what they really were, and what they desperately tried to make me—an honest, God-fearing person.

"I came to understood that all my pursuits in life had been in vain. They inevitably involved gains of the body or gains of the pocket. There was nothing spiritual about them at all.

"Then I met Leah, and...here we are."

After he had finished telling us his story, we sat in silence, each of us looking at the man before us. The rabbi softly interrupted our thoughts with a painful reminder.

"Your story is most touching, Mr. Meisels. Personally, I believe your every word. However, and it pains me to have to tell you this again, we need some form of evidence proving to us beyond reasonable doubt that you are who you claim. And that evidence must be nothing less than two Jews who can vouch for you."

"Isn't Mr. Kahan's presence enough to convince you?" asked Leah. Before the rabbi could answer this question, Mr. Kahan put his finger up as if to stress a point.

"I represent a painful part of this fellow's life, rabbi. His family and mine have been on friendly terms for many years. When I planned to come out here, they begged me to find him and send him their love and hope that he would return to them. When I arrived, I investigated his whereabouts only to discover that he'd changed his name and was living outside of Melbourne.

I arranged to travel out to his property, but by chance ran across him one night. He wouldn't recall this meeting because he was as drunk as a dog. I was so disgusted with the stories he told, particularly those describing how tasty snake and possum meat is, that I thought there was no hope left. I ran into him the following day on one of the main corners in town and spat at his feet. He turned as white as a bone. I frightened the living daylights out of him.

"I wrote back to his parents saying I hadn't seen him. I never thought they'd write back. I assumed they would give up all hope. But they didn't. Not only did they write again requesting me not to give up in my search for him, but they sent some of his things as well."

Out of his jacket pocket he pulled a picture and a bundle of papers and placed them on the desk in front of him.

"Here is a daguerreotype of Yankel Meisels and his family, taken many years ago."

Matthews's hand dashed out to the desk. He picked up the daguerreotype and held it close to his face. His eyes welled up with tears. He passed it around to the other members in the room. The picture alone was enough to convince me that he was telling the truth. Not only did the man sitting before us look like the young man in the daguerreotype, but he looked like his father's identical twin.

As the daguerreotype made its way around the room, Mr. Kahan picked up a document from among the papers. It was a money order.

"This piece of paper might help your investigation," he said. "Your parents sent me this money order for twenty pounds, which you must sign in order to claim the sum. Sign it!" he demanded.

Meisels picked up a pen and signed his name on the slip of paper. Mr. Kahan then picked up one of the other papers and studied it carefully.

"Look, rabbi! The signatures are identical. This man can only be Yankel Meisels."

Rabbi Rintel's face showed no signs of the same excitement Mr. Kahan's had. "I'm sorry, Mr. Kahan. It's still not halachically permissible. We need one more witness."

Mr. Kahan seemed oblivious to this request and persisted in pressing his case for the similar signatures. He quite lost control of himself until Rabbi Rintel, no longer able to listen to such useless appeals, brought his hand down on the table. The third bang imposed a silence to the room.

"Mr. Kahan. Again, I will tell you that according to Jewish law we need two witnesses proving this man is Jewish. You are one. We therefore need one more."

It took Mr. Kahan a moment or two to truly comprehend, but when he did, he slapped his right thigh with his open hand.

"Rabbi Rintel, I'm on my way back to Sydney. I've reserved a seat on a coach due to leave at seven this evening. I'm traveling with a man recently immigrated to Australia from England. He knows this man's family. Give me leave and I'll return here within the hour."

After an anxious hour spent mostly in gloomy silence, Kahan returned, accompanied by an elderly man.

"Gentlemen," announced Mr. Kahan as he re-entered the room, "allow me to introduce Dr. Josef Herman." Without giving this Dr. Herman a chance to shake hands, Mr. Kahan came immediately to the point. "Look at him long, sir, and may your memory serve us well."

"Your face is familiar, sir," he said, addressing Meisels. "Many years ago my services were requested by your parents. I came to your house where I found you ill and delirious. I suppose that's why you don't recognize me. But it's you all right. Yes, gentlemen, this is Yankel Meisels. If I may prove the point beyond doubt, I distinctly recall a brown birth mark above one of your elbows.

A look of relief came over Meisels, who quickly rolled up his right sleeve and proudly displayed a brown birth mark precisely where Dr. Herman had said it was.

Cries of *mazel tov* rang through the room. In my excitement I hugged Yankel and nearly squeezed the breath out of him.

The excitement and happiness that erupted after the *chuppah* took place were extraordinary—quite Australian in character, I'd say. Leah looked splendid, and Yankel danced with boundless energy. Members of our family rejoiced until late into the evening. They were accompanied by Mr. Kahan, who seemed to find the strength to outdance us without a pause, and who, after the band had stopped playing, continued to dance on.

A month after the wedding, Yankel and Leah sailed to England where Yankel reconciled himself with his family. After two years absence they returned to Australia with his parents. They and their dear family live in Melbourne, not far from us.

The bonds between Yankel and I are stronger today than ever. These days we have more to share together. With no material needs to pursue, we sit in Rabbi Rintel's office day after day poring over the Chumash, *mishnayos*, and Gemara. Leah has become a wonderful housewife and appears to have calmed down in nature, content to tend to her family and take an active part in community affairs.

But we are an anomaly in this part of the world. Apart from the rabbi and ourselves, few other members of the community share our desire and fervor for Torah. Unfortunately, it is this last point, the lack of dedication to Yiddishkeit, which has served as the catalyst for the writing of this journal.

I have been in this country for nearly thirty years now. The longer I stay, the more concern I feel about the future of my descendants. Australia has provided us with a warm, peaceful climate to live in. For many it is the Garden of Eden. There are no overcrowding and poor standards of living as there are in England. The promise of infinite opportunity is endless, and all it takes is a man with endeavor and enterprise to capitalize on them. Yet men here run around as they do in any other city of the world, blinkered by the sight of riches. Nothing else matters but the pot at the end of every potential rainbow.

This is fine for most men. We Jews, however, are made of a different mettle. Whether we admit it or not, or even if we are aware of it or not, we cannot run from the fact that there is in every one of us *tzelem Elokim*. We possess a mission higher than building a bigger bank balance or a more lavish home.

Today, despite my wealth, honored position, and great satisfaction in life, I am a man desperately afraid. Though my son received a strong Jewish education from me, it could be that after I have left this world he will succumb to the pressures of this godless colony and maintain only what observance he feels is comfortable in what he terms "this modern age." What will he pass down to his son? And what will be passed down to future generations?

Already, so many cut themselves off from their brethren. Marriages between Jews and non-Jews are all too common.

I am a man who lives with the fear that somewhere, generations down the line, my family is going to take the same course that so many other Jews have taken. I am terrified that my children won't have the available tools to pass Torah on to their children, as I have passed Torah on to them.

As I write this, my son Yaakov is planning to move

northwest with his family and settle himself away from the noise of this busy city. His intentions are good, for he wants to take the bastion of Torah into the wild, collecting lost Jews as he goes. He has already persuaded five families to travel with him. Yet how long will it be before his ideals fall into the abyss of this vast land?

I feel the seeds of assimilation being sown among my own grandchildren. They are lurking, waiting for the years ahead to attack their defenseless prey.

I, Moses Lazar, pray that this journal has found its way into deserving hands. I pray that the same values and beliefs I hold today will be held by you, my dear reader, progeny of my body and soul. Help save the children of your generation from tumbling downward. *Bnei Yisrael* reached the forty-ninth level of impurity before being brought out of Egypt, and if, so soon after their departure, they reached the highest level of holiness at Sinai, I at least live with the comfort of mind that all hope is not lost. I pray that you, too, will act with speed and concern and doctor these lost souls.

Chazak VeAmatz,

Moses Lazar
Melbourne, 1879

Epilogue

Moshe gently closed the book and reached out for the menorah. How it sparkled in the rays of the afternoon sun.

An enormous sense of joy suddenly welled up within him. The link to the past that had eluded him all his life had finally been uncovered.

He had often wondered at the term so easily given to him and others like him: *ba'al teshuvah*. I knew nothing before I became observant, he would say, so where is my *teshuvah*? How can I return to a place I've never been?

And now he knew. He was not a rootless wanderer, treading unexplored paths in a search for the unknown. His life of Torah had been lived before, by his very own kin. He was merely rediscovering truths that his ancestors had always known and lived by.

Even more than the solid gold menorah that he

would proudly display in his Jerusalem home, this newfound sense of belonging was his legacy from Moses Lazar. He was thankful for it, grateful that he had merited such an inheritance, and ready to accept the responsibilities that it entailed. He would redouble his efforts in learning, and ultimately go out to "doctor the lost souls," as his great-great-grandfather had requested of him.

More than a bequest, he had inherited a mission.